THE CROSSFIRE OF LOVE

"Contemporary characters with deep internal conflicts and fractured souls. The book is a provocative read that inspired me to introspect and heal myself."

– Abhinav Kashyap
Director, *Dabangg*

"...has a flair for lucid writing that at once captivates the reader. I wish more power to his creativity."

– Ramesh Vinayak
Executive Editor, *Hindustan Times, Chandigarh*

"...a juicy novel that makes a fine reading... writer's ability to craft well his thought process with flights of imagination. The elements of curiosity and euphoria make the book interesting and thrilling..."

– Arvind Singh Bisht
Former UP state information commissioner &
Political editor of *The Times of India*

"There are no dragons in reality, but plenty when you decode the shocking ending. Go for this one, you'll be a fan."

– Gurpreet Singh Chhina
Times Now

"Addictive and edgy. The twists and turns keep on feeding on your curiosity... a real page turner. The arc of major characters is so realistically volatile, the romance is so passionate and the heartbreaks are shocking. The moment you are done, you'd want to read it all over again!"

– Abhishek Sharma
Author & Celebrity Photographer

THE CROSSFIRE OF LOVE

DHIREN TIWARI

Srishti
PUBLISHERS & DISTRIBUTORS

SRISHTI PUBLISHERS & DISTRIBUTORS
Registered Office: N-16, C.R. Park
New Delhi – 110 019
Corporate Office: 212A, Peacock Lane
Shahpur Jat, New Delhi – 110 049
editorial@srishtipublishers.com

First published by
Srishti Publishers & Distributors in 2020

10 9 8 7 6 5 4 3 2 1

Printed and bound in India

To the silence
that broke into #meToo

Acknowledgement

What words can we not say to keep the world calm?

I have tried to write something different, yet powerful, that'd leave the tread marks in our muddy thoughts much after all the pages were turned, the book stacked and the night lamp darkened.

Whether I succeeded or not, you'll decide, but there are many special people who helped me shape this thought-provoking story.

A huge thanks to Mike Garrett, who is also credited as the first editor of Stephen King! Mike doesn't accept a whole lot of manuscripts. He was gracious enough to accept this one, and his comments and critique made a huge impact to tighten the plot and to sparkle it with crispier language.

Heartiest gratitude to Mr Abhinav Kashyap, whose powerful writing and sharp creative acumen continues to inspire me everyday.

Special thanks to Arup Bose from Srishti Publishers for taking on the challenge of getting this unique story to the readers. A huge shout out to Stuti Sharma for her insightful critique and excellent edits.

A slew of inspiring authors, but foremost are Stieg Larsson, Paula Hawkins, Gillian Flynn, and of course, Sidney Sheldon.

A sugar-laced special thanks to my wife, Ashi, for sticking by, albeit with that hard frozen wide-eyed stare. It still haunts me.

My kids – Vihaan and Suhana – are my life, and while they can't read the contents until they are of age, their excitement towards my writing is dangerously contagious! Words like, "you only have 100 more pages, daddy," kept me going even after exhausting 16-hour work days.

A very special thanks to the rock solid support from my brothers (Virendra and Hirendra), my sisters-in-law (Sony and Babita), my beautiful nieces (Jia and Shagun) and an energetic nephew (Veer).

Thank you to Satya Pandey, my mother-in-law, for your kind words and positive encouragement.

A huge thanks to all the early readers, friends and well-wishers for your inspiring comments and continuous support! Special mentions to Rishi Kwatra for always being there.

I can't thank my parents enough. They have been publicizing my first novel (*Punk Sunk Love*) in the Hindi heartland of India, well realizing the limitations of English language outreach in the area. Thank you for your relentless passion. It's because of it that I keep writing. So, thank you, again!

Saira

The hot southerly wind did not intend to slow down even at 8 p.m. in Old Delhi. Air conditioning was as rare as a white giraffe in this pumpkin-coloured motel. In the room, the lone window threw open, filling the room with foul odour from the pulpy streets below.

I could feel her presence under the bleeding sky. The Pison; born from my own flesh, firing from her burning eyes, lunging her five slimy legs through my meat, shredding it with her spikey antlers. Mercilessly, she'd crawl on my arms, and like a leak in a copper pipe, she'd snake on my neck, under my cheeks, to the left of my nose, then spring into my eyes, boom!

She'd wait there, throbbing before ripping through my bloody eyes and crawling straight out of my skin, leaving me in a pool of shame; then, she'd start again, then again, and again. *I want this to stop. This is not a dream.*

It's happening right now.

I needed to shake Pison off. *Someone, please take the red tape off my eyes!*

I waggled my wrists tied against the rustic metal bed headboard. My whole body convulsed in yet another failed attempt. Sweat splashed on my legs, my thighs, my hips, and my back. I felt like a pig dressed for her slaughter in a soaking pink corset.

The dense oak smell of bubbly champagne sparked hope once more. *I wish I can drink it.* However, that champagne wasn't for me. It was for the creepy Supreme Court judge throbbing his illness of rape, and I, his strappy inmate in a rotten cell – all a part of his sick fantasy.

Slow creaking sound of the door rang like the first strike from a war bugle. *He is out!* The moldy smell of his naked torso lodged like a bullet. So did the sound of his grinding teeth, seemingly spiced with the arousal of what he was going to do to me.

"I never saw you without clothes, you know," he growled. "Such a rich fawn skin, hourglass shape… you're my own Kim Kardashian." His breath stretched like the tongue of a bell. "I'm afraid I'm going to hurt you today. I hope you don't mind."

His heavy steps echoed louder, and louder, and then no more. *What will I do when he's on me?*

"Strapping my pigtail like a collar rope, he slithered his slimy tongue on my bare legs.

I wished him dead. I wished me dead. *Someone save me, please. I won't get into this trap again.* His barbaric, hairy arms dug inside my bra, and my scream stabbed through the tape on my mouth. "Would you like to go to wonderland?"

A bright thud, shiny lights, doors opened, and the camera was live. My face blurred out, but not my legs. The vulgarity with which the TV camera zoomed on them shredded all the journalist principles the crew avowed.

I'd been dolled up and hung like a mermaid for dozens of these exposé. There was always an element of danger, but what happened today was out of bounds. *Neil has to answer for it.*

As my shield soldered back into culture in an adjacent room, the judge had nowhere to hide. All his prestige stripped in a single stroke. *How can men be so sick? All of them, including Neil.*

"What you see today is justice; justice by people. A corrupt judge, who trades in an ill fantasy with a young girl for a rapist's bail," Neil's repulsive voice echoed from the TV.

"You nailed it, Saira. This story is huge!" Neil bellowed as he barged into my room. He stood on the stairs, trying not to look shorter than me. His frizzy locks flowering an extra inch to his height. He needed all the boosters he could get his hands on.

"Do me a favour. Don't put too much clothes on you. I'll take it off in an hour anyway." His mouth foamed with lust.

What does he think those comments make me feel? I don't think he cares much about my feelings. Actually, he doesn't think. Period. He's a man in a world made by men.

"That's not why I'm still shacked up in this filthy motel." I shunned him.

"Sorry. My bad. What was so urgent that couldn't wait an hour?"

"Do you realize how close it got today?" I implored. "He was on me. Why didn't you come sooner?"

"We were just waiting for the safe word."

"I had tape on my mouth and that was supposed to be the last resort, Neil."

His brows curled him into an all-too-familiar counterfeit. "I'm sorry," he said, but I'd tell he didn't mean a single word of it. "Listen, I have to go live again, but I promise you, I'll give an earful to the team. You're right! How could they let this happen to you? I might even fire someone for this."

He patiently waited to hear from me. "I won't leave until you forgive me," he continued.

"Last time. Okay," I said after much thought, finally giving in to his truce.

"Of course. Now go home and rest." His hands reached my hips, but quickly retracted. "I'll see you later." His politeness was back, even if just for this moment.

The walk from the bus station to my apartment felt waxed in nostalgia about my first encounter with shame on this street five years ago.

I thought I'd be perfectly safe. After all, the building was squarely in the middle of a marketplace, crowded on all sides with vegetable hawkers, butcher shops, restaurants, and even a police post.

Perpetrators, however, brood in crowded places too. They'd slip in, run their dirty hands on top of the clothes, and when the crowd thickened, they'd even grope from under it.

Each day, every step I took, a bell rang in my ears, cautioning, me to look down and walk away. At least you aren't raped... At least you aren't raped.

My anger popped like the cork of a shaken champagne bottle. I unhooked my phone and live shamed that son of a bitch on YouTube.

"Look at those pigs, giving media bytes as if they caught this animal." A young girl had said soon after. "You are so brave. This animal did this to #MeToo."

My head had beamed higher, much higher. I hadn't realized, how my life was about to change when a stranger had introduced soon thereafter. "I am Neil, the host of 'Monsters among us'."

"Thanks for forgiving me." Neil moaned as we lay together in his bed.

"Thank the landlord who cut my water supply."

"I owe him a dinner then." His occasional silliness reminded me of the first time we made love.

It was in my drought-struck dingy apartment, the night of my first exposé. Unfazed by months of failed attempts to buy me even a cup of coffee, he was calm. That night, however, was different.

He volunteered to clean my dishes, even vacuumed the flat. He then patiently listened to all of my excitement. Smiled at the right times, laughed at all my jokes. He was my little dude. It was before his sleazy hands dug inside my skirt. I guess I was sleazy too. I didn't stop him when he pulled my skirt below my knees or when he ripped my underwear. My first lovemaking; his first too, with me.

"You really know how to do this," he had lauded to me right after. I took that as a compliment, a girl who knew how to please her man. He seemingly mistook it for my quirk, as if I wanted to dance in this muck every time we had sex.

He'd done it right now as well, parroting to me. "You really know how to do this."

"What is 'this'?"

"You know, what we just did."

"Say it. Out loud."

"Fuck."

"What's wrong with you? Don't use the word *fuck*. I don't like it; it's so gross."

"But you asked me to say it out loud."

"I wanted to know what it meant to you." *He thinks of me no more than that chair lying there, I guess.*

"I didn't mean that at all. I meant it was lovemaking."

"See? You could have said that at first. But your primal taste is just a hard fuck, bent over, again and again."

"Phew, that's totally uncalled for. You know what? You're right. I'm sorry." He was back to zipping his pants, abandoning me in the bed like a soiled sheet.

"You think somehow I am meat bait in real life, too. Don't you?" I fought back.

"No." He didn't even dare look me in the eye.

"Enough. It's your turn now. Give me what you promised." I couldn't let him just take whatever he wanted from me.

"Is this what our relationship is to you?" he questioned.

"Of course, now that you've gotten what you wanted, you're getting all poetic."

"Alright, I'll talk to Suri first chance I get."

"Not first chance; first thing. Tomorrow."

Amaan

The sky above me tore from the middle, unleashing a horde of lighted snakes, their silver-heads jarred with hisses. But the Skinhead stood stoic, his naked torso welded to his legs, his feet iced in the ground.

"Let me tell you a little secret." Skinhead's voice didn't waver. "Death isn't the end."

His frosty words painted to spook, and so far, he was winning. I was the loser muddy fox gripping grass for a husky wolf.

"You understand what needs to be done, right?" He stood untamed. The plot to kill him sprouted like weed in my head. All I had to do was to take ten lousy steps. He'd pounce to grab me, I slide out of the way, and off he'd go down the ten-thousand-feet fall straight into the blue water lake. Not even the water could save him from this steep fall. *Maybe he'll die even before he hits the water, his head crushed by the grand volcano glasses spiked around this mountain.*

"This black mountain has been dormant since before Jesus Christ. There's no volcano that's going to furnace to your help."

His menacing eyes seemingly plunged in my head, and my clever scheme once again choked in his fear.

It was clear. I had to crunch my knees to his demand, unless, of course, the neon blue blood in my muscles reignited. *How can I become the warrior my father declared I could never be?*

Just this thought of my father, and the insults baked fresh.

"What a shame." That was my father's verdict, a decade ago, in front of hundreds of guests, denouncing every grain of royal blood in me. The cause: I had fell off the horse during my 'blue blood' ceremony, a dramatic name for fifteenth birthday, celebrating the first step in real manhood, which in my case wasn't much of a celebration.

I had become the child whom my father wanted to hide. It didn't bother him one leaf that the public humiliation had turned me into a certified weirdo right in that moment. Instead, his breath was doused with all the whores' tongues.

"Listen to him, Amaan." My brother Veer's whispers brought me back to the black mountain. "We don't have much time." I listened to my brother as his muscular jaw flaunted with words. His likeness to my father was remarkable. I had trained myself to ignore it. It wasn't his fault if his face moved the same or that he had farmed similar knotless black silk hair pulled like a shiny veil from the temple all the way to the neck.

"Come here, my little brother." He pulled me in, dwarfing me under his iron arms, and while his eyes poured a deluge, a question dawned. *Why is my face as dry as a yellow desert dune?*

"I'm here for you. Never forget that." He looked down, not out of disrespect, or that I was short at six feet; he was just taller.

"It's time." The Skinhead priest made his presence known again.

I had to gather the courage to say goodbye. *I can't. I won't.*

"It's customary that you must be the one," Skinhead advised to an arousing quiver that swallowed my face. "You have to make it quick, or you have to do it in front of thousands more of your own people."

The brown-clad police officers, not one or two, but trucks full of them were charging up the serpentine black mountain highway, behind them a silent gap, then a giant roaring tail of Attanoogians covering every pebble of the road from the mountain, to the lake, and to the gates of Attanooga.

"Your sculpted dimpled face, your bouffant hair, even the mole above your lips... your mysterious resemblance to the late queen Sana is for a reason." Skinhead spewed a hailstorm again. "Not just because you are her son, but because you are the chosen one."

"Tradition mandates that you light your mother's pyre." My soul revolted against his ghastly remarks. "She'll watch you through her soul as you set her free. Once free, she'll forever guard you from the stars."

"That thought is a powerful remedy." Veer's wet eyes shrunk in admittance. *I have to let go.*

The memories of the past were clearing up. Before I could indulge any further in my delusions of the past, the screeching halt of the first batch of police cars drifted my attention.

"Sir, the crowd is getting closer." The police commissioner's urgent words immediately got my brother's attention, but something else got mine. "Ah. I didn't notice you, Your Highness.

I haven't seen those deep blue eyes in a decade. Regal, like your mother, our late queen." He had found an awkward moment to lionize me.

"Don't forget that Amaan's six feet frame is built of solid iron, much like our father," Veer added.

The police commissioner apologetically replied, "Yes, of course, Your Highness."

"How far is the crowd?" Veer steered back to the point.

"Ten minutes tops," the police commissioner said.

"Do we have all the barricades deployed?"

"We do, sir." The commissioner hesitated.

"Then what's the urgency?"

"Sir, our arrangements can control a few thousand people," he said, then waved his arms to the road down the hill.

"They're upset. It's their queen. We'll let the barriers lose," Veer declared.

"That will be catastrophic, sir," the commissioner quickly snapped back. "You already know what's happening outside the prison."

"Which prison?" I asked.

"The prison where your father's killer, Durga is lodged."

"Isn't he supposed to be hanged in a few months?" I asked.

"In my opinion, it would be a good social service if that bastard was killed by the mob," Veer minced. "But what has that got to do with the funeral here?" he queried.

"The superstition is staggering, sir. Just like they think Durga's action started this town's descent, they believe that offering last prayers to the queen would do some sort of miracle and rid them of their distress."

"Distress?" I whispered.

The vacuum of all these years was finally catching up to me.

The police commissioner continued. "Sir, a lot has changed. Half of the town has been destroyed."

"You don't need to worry about it." Veer interrupted to discard his concern. "This is my constituency and my people. They're not animals to be kept away in cages."

I couldn't gather whether it was his remorse speaking or his greed for admiration as a politician. I was kicked to the side again.

"I'd like to do it in solitary," I appealed.

I couldn't say what annoyed Veer more, my interruption or my intention. His eyes dotted the laser directly at Skinhead's, who for a change had softened his gums in a rare agreement with me.

"Sure." Veer paused. "Of course."

"Once the pyre is lit, we can open the gates, sir," the commissioner assured. "And the chopper will take you back to the palace."

The moment was now real. I had run out of time. This was the last chance to see my mother before I burned her to ashes. I felt my muscles turning to slush.

"May god be with you." Skinhead declared in a uniquely moist voice. *My death dealer has gone soft.*

Chants sparked in the air as I limped the ritualistic seven laps around my mother's sandalwood pyre. Every lap I took filled me with imagery of the times she cared for me, fought for me, rebelled for me, broke for me, smiled for me. Only I wished that my father didn't ruin her beautiful moments with his ugliness. Alas, even in this pledge for mercy, he had managed to sit in.

"Here you go, Your Highness." The Skinhead priest handed over the ginger head torch, growling in golden flames. *The arsonist of the modern death, trading in bodies for arson.*

"Remember one rule," my mother used to say. "Nature makes us; nurture also makes us. You just have to choose one." *Today I want to choose my nature, but I can't, Mom. Can I? Answer me! Please! Tell me!"*

"Hurry, Your Highness," the commissioner pleaded. "The crowd is only minutes away."

All my barrels of tactics were gone and I had to do one thing I hoped I never would. I threw the torch into her body.

Veer stood steadfast by me. Wind blowing through his armored chest didn't bother him. "Don't you see it, Amaan? Mom died two days ago on the same date as our father's ten years ago."

I felt like screaming atop a lighthouse. *Don't bring him into this. Let this be her place.* All the words deployed, the sentences were wreathed, but instead I found myself floating into a morning in Manhattan seven days ago.

"Remember, Amaan, you see the world like no one else does, but that doesn't mean the world will see you the same way, were my mother's morning words to me that day in our Park Avenue apartment.

In the morning, after her bath, she let the nurse go early. I didn't understand why, but gave up the thought of slightest resistance when her frail smile creased. "I want fresh air," she demanded right after, and I opened the sky windows.

"I want to smoke," she requested in mischief, and I ran down the stairs, barged onto the street, fell on my way, stood right up, ran inside bodega, grabbed a pack of Marlboro Ultralights, and in a puff of a smoke I was back, sitting by her side, a lit cigarette gliding in her hands.

More than the desire to smoke, she admired the look of it in her hands. She dragged just one puff. "I can't be bad anymore, I guess," she said. "It's been two decades since the last one."

Today, however, was different. An eerie feeling danced around me, whispering, "Get through today, then everything would be fine. She would be fine." I was ready to believe that stage four leukemia would disappear on its own. I was ready to pluck the moon, plow the fields, build a rocket, or dive like an eagle. Whatever it took.

I sledged until the last rod of light vanished from the sky and the cuckoo emerged from the wall to crow twelve hoots. The day had passed. I was done with my part of the bargain. Now, it was god's turn to turn my prophecy green.

"You look radiant, Mommy." Her face sparkled the next morning. She hadn't coughed blood all night. Who says miracles don't exist?

"I brewed green tea for you," I exclaimed.

"Come here, my son." She scooched up the head rail. "You're an angel. My perfect prince."

"What about Veer then?"

"You're lucky to have a brother like him. Go to India. Stay with him. Listen to him."

"For what?" I was clueless at the turn of our conversation.

She, however, chose not to reply. She knew I felt insulted, but that didn't bother her. How could she ignore me? I couldn't tolerate that. She had to answer. Period.

Okay, I'd let the nurse return from the lobby, and I'd live the same routine over and over again. All she had to do was answer me. Was it that hard?

"What have you done, Amaan?" the nurse screamed. She had managed to fool the security guards and, through her spare key, barged right into the apartment. "Let go, please," she pleaded.

"Let go of what?"

"She's in a better place."

I wanted to laugh at her, taunt her, but my mother had raised me better. Does she think mother is dead? She had no idea that I made a pact with god. God doesn't lie. Everyone knows that.

"Guard us, our queen. Attanooga has lost its sheen. Guard us, our queen..." The howling of the mob snatched me back. *I have to hide. I have to run.* I couldn't stand in the open, exposing my softest emotions, so what if thousands of her fans, pupils of her kingdom, felt the same. Emotions are weird neurosis in us humans. Some hide in pride, like my brother; some burn in rage, like the people of Attanooga; *and some itch for a kill, like me.*

Two Months Later

Amaan

"You haven't stepped out of this filth in two months." Veer's footsteps splintered the clumsy wooden floors. "I had two flat tires on the dirt road to this dump," he said. His entourage of servants, bodyguards, and advisors spread behind him like a Chinese fan.His own face rinsed clean of glee.

"You should get some charcoal on the road," I said.

"I thought about it." He smirked just as his servant unfolded a chair for him to sit. *Who carries his own furniture?* "I'd rather let this place rot and crumble than to refurbish it into a disgraced tourist spot." His cheeks hived, as if bitten by pollen. He didn't seem to care about the porous red cedar walls or the twenty feet high vaulted Douglas fir ceiling. It was all dust to him.

"What do they call it now?" I looked up to the one hundred and twenty candles crystal chandelier. A bipolar feeling of shame and joy chaffed me. "The murdered wolf cottage?"

The entire staff behind Veer instantly dropped their heads like a slinky.

"It's a shame, I can't demolish this. I will, though, as soon as Durga is hanged," he bemoaned.

Unlike Veer's inordinate abomination for the cottage, it was the only place where the shrapnel of my brain didn't explode.

Veer's eyes slanted to the man-size skylight windows above us. "Look outside. All you see is trees grown in gloom and infested with bad memories. Come back to the palace," he insisted, scolding off the voices climbing up my hair. "At least the phones work in the palace. You don't have to punish yourself." He paused, signaling his staff to leave us alone. "Last time you were in this state, it split our family. I'd like us to be stronger than ever now. Our people need us."

"I didn't split our family," I said. Each word fell harder than the previous one.

"That's not what I meant." He paused, seemingly to breathe a fresh thought. "You know what? It doesn't matter. Mother is with our father now, in heaven, watching, as the justice will be noosed around our father's killer."

"A man who wore loyalty like a badge, only to thrash it and butcher the master," I said.

"Listen. Our father always believed in you, you know." His forceful compliments smelled worse than the dead black boar in the kitchen. "I'll have the staff pack your bags. You are moving to the palace. You don't have to hunt your food anymore."

"I like hunting," I replied.

"Then come here and hunt whenever you want. Just don't hoister here in this pig-smelling dump."

"I won't. I need to go back to New York." I set my desire free.

"I don't think that's such a good idea." Veer disagreed. "Mother's memories will be a lot harder to erase when you're in a place where you lived with her for ten years." *Who says anything about erasing memory? Why is he talking to me like that?*

"I like New York. There's a certain air to it," I said.

He didn't move. His eyes just stood there in high beam, blinding everyone who dared, but not a pinch in them.

"Please, I do need to go," I begged.

"You know what our mother said before she died?" he said. "Think of Amaan not as your brother, but as your son. Do everything that you'd do for your son."

Suddenly, my mother's oval face flamed in the still air, hushing me to listen to Veer, then vanished like an ice cube in hell's boiling pan.

"What else did she say?" My interest piqued.

"She said that you'd not take this well; that is, if she was gone. And to remind you that nurturing can fix flaws we can't even see." The stench of his words churned my stomach. My innards gnarled. *Did she tell him everything? Why is he so prescriptive in his words? Breathe. Relax. Don't let the paranoia get to you. I need to run. No I don't. I need to get some air.*

"I'll come back." My words paled.

"Are you feeling okay?" he asked.

"Must be the acids," I digressed. "But I do need to go back to New York," I insisted. "I have unfinished work. I need to make sure I serve my notice period at the hospital and wrap up a few things."

"I thought you left med school?"

"I did," I replied. "I volunteer for my professor."

"Okay. How much time do you need?"

"One month tops."

He stayed mum until his smile violated the agreement. "As you wish, my brother. I'll tell the staff to make all the arrangements." He paused. "And remember, I'll always be there for you."

"Thanks, brother," I said, my stomach still coiled with anxiety.

I walked out to the balcony; his iron steps followed.

The cold wind slapped my face, squashing the demons back to the caves. My face once again sprouted life.

"You see this valley?" Veer said, sticking his neck out of the bushes of hairy mountain range under which this cottage lay besieged. Our eyes rolled down the hill to the town of Attanooga, and in it lay neatly stacked houses with identical red terracotta roofs, every house painted in white, streets pacing with horseback carts.

"This was the first planned town of this country, much before there was really 'the country'," Veer droned.

"I'm sure that with your chief minister nomination, you'll restore the glory once again."

He smirked with an immature pride. "Haven't gotten yet."

"But it's all over the news."

"Conjecture like these are good in politics." That's all he suggested on that topic.

Saira

It wasn't even 10 a.m.; the tea man was still doing his rounds, peeking into cubes, trying to find warm bodies to buy tea. "It's Monday, the Zombie day. They won't be here until noon," I informed him. His bleak smile returned and off he ran to the elevators.

"Saira?" The thorny voice of channel head Suri calling my name was a recurring clip in my dreams, but not today. Blood in my ravines gushed fast; pink confetti flushed my face.

Ask me something that I want. *Like, hey Saira, how about I get you your own show? Or something like, I have Neil tied up to the urinal, and why don't you beat the shit out of him?*

"You're from Attanooga, correct?" His unimaginative question cost all my excitement a bloodless death.

"Yes. I did some schooling there," I replied coldly.

"Do you have a few minutes to chat?"

"Sure."

"Why don't we go into my office?"

All my hopes crushed, and I wasn't dressing up another tizzy anytime soon.

"So here's the deal." Suri carefully closed the door of his office. "Sit, relax!"

I did sit, but didn't relax. I couldn't relax.

"We're doing a limited series." He flicked a report over to me. "Read it."

"Think of this, as the last royal romance in India." He paused, quite absurdly actually, perhaps waiting for a sugar-dotted nod. *How dumb does he think I am?* My body sat still, but my flesh was throbbing. Wasn't sure if it was the anticipation of excitement or fear of all this turning to a shameless request.

Suri continued. "Did you know that two months ago, it was the tenth death anniversary of His Highness Rudra Singh?" His sudden pause-and-stare routine spooked me. "And coincidentally, on the same day, his wife died too."

"Yes!" I conferred a deep acknowledgment, quite contrary to the fact that he could be talking about cat videos and I'd have reacted the same.

"How well are you still connected to Attanooga?"

"I try not to stay in touch." I said, not letting a single chip of that place's dreariness defect into my years' worth of hard-earned solace.

"You may want to rethink that." He looked straight at me like an honorable man, not looking below my neck, but above it. "We have plans to do a story on it."

The horns and teeth of Attanooga had already begun to pounce memories out of my past. The nausea, the repulsive smell; it was all coming back. *I need to stop this.*

"Stop my existing work?" I asked. My anxiety rolled up, squeezed into a bundle of nerves.

"Yes," he said after a long dragging thought, which came wrapped in a smile. My nerves swiftly untangled.

"But I don't understand? This is like a documentary piece." I quickly moved past the embarrassment.

"Depends on how you look at it." He stood to draw his thoughts. "I see a couple of mystery angles here. First, let's look at the king, Rudra Singh, killed by his own driver. Don't you wonder why? Second, after his death, his wife never sets foot in India even once, and then dies a symbolic death on the same day as her husband.

"Her popularity, by the way, is another animal of its own. They had to call reserve forces to control the crowd on her funeral, and even that didn't work." He paused, seemingly to embellish in his art of creating conspiracy out of thin air. He continued, "The cause of her death could be another jewel in the crown. Was her death natural, or not?"

"It is a bit of a stretch." I bit my own tongue just to punish myself. *Why did I say that? Come back you stupid words.*

"Why?" he asked, and he had no wrinkles of frustration, so different from Neil.

"What I remember of the queen, she was immensely popular, and I don't know if throwing her into muck is going to work."

I thought and said, "How do we dig this up anyway? To your point, all the major players are dead and cremated."

"Those are the right questions, but you or whosoever takes this show would need to get an answer to."

Did he just say, you? "I'll do it." That's all I could proffer, in that very moment. All my cringe for Attanooga muffled to death, or coma, at the very least.

Suri smiled. I felt as if my consent wasn't a surprise for him. He must have seen worse, girls selling their souls to get a show. "I've seen your career plan. Every year you've expressed a desire to host your own show. So, here is your chance."

This moment wasn't an imagination anymore. But it had that unwelcome feeling, the one that came with the smell of Attanooga. However, in this moment I didn't care. I wanted to do something crazy, exciting.

All my excitement rusted away when Neil came in unannounced.

"Thanks for coming over, Neil." Suri, too, lost all the high places in my mind. "Neil will be your mentor." He paused. I hoped he was having second thoughts about putting Neil in all this. "Think of him like a springboard. He will help get you through all the nuances of running a show." He looked at Neil sincerely. "It was Neil's recommendation actually."

I wanted to look at Neil in sincerity, but I couldn't. For some reason, my gut reminded me that the relationship with Neil was a mistake. I should have dealt with a strict heart from the beginning, not just for the past two months. His countless pleadings shredded in the trash, his flowers returned, and his text messages marked as spam.

"Very nice." That's all I could sass.

"It was," Neil said. "A personal conflict equals emotion equals an explosive story."

"I don't understand?" I conceded after a long awkward silence.

"Let me explain," Suri interjected. "The first story of this series needs to be personal, close, scandalous and juicy.

"This is your town, your people. And you have an 'in' with the royal family."

"Sure," I replied. His statement was part true. I did have an in, but not anymore. *Maybe I should tell him that. Wait. What if he decides to punt this to someone else?*

"When do we plan to go live with this?" I asked.

"We want to do this on Dusshera, the biggest festival celebration at Attanooga," Suri declared.

"That shouldn't be a problem." Neil surmised. He had to spill his filth, hoping his pretense of faithfulness would erase months of cockiness.

"I understand and I'm ready. Let me finalize the point of view then," I said.

Neil sneered again. I couldn't bear him anymore. I really wanted to punch him. "We have all that sorted. Why don't you and I discuss this later today?" Another tragic attempt of his to work late and try to get into my skirt. I felt bad for him.

"Sure. I'll set up some time." I droned.

"Alright, Saira." Suri stood to shake my hands. "You're going to join the big league now! I can only imagine how tall your career is going to grow with this."

"Thank you, Suri."

"Remember one thing, Saira. What we can sell is sex, shame and shock. Get me that with this story and you'll be famous!" Suri's parting words peeled as an orange, and so did my chi.

Amaan

"You don't worry Amaan, I am here now," Veer said. Just his presence calmed my last six hours of swollen nerves in the detention room located three levels underground at the Delhi airport.

The foul mold smell in the room claimed its second victim. "Why do you have my brother locked in this grungy..." His sneeze ate the last of his words.

It took him a split second to recompose his rhythm. "This is unnecessary," Veer announced to the authorities paying no attention to the giant white circular FBI imprint on the glass wall. "My brother here is a diplomat and, as such, FBI has no jurisdiction." His remarks were unwavering.

"We have to run this interrogation through its due course," the FBI officer announced.

"Then, here is the notice of representation, and the only way you get to Amaan is through me." He and I sneezed again within seconds of each other. The dust mites in the room seemingly added fuel to his already simmering rage. "In addition, stay tuned for a lawsuit, because you threw my brother out of a plane for saving the life of a steward? Explain that to the public in *due course*."

"We would still need a statement from your brother, sir." The FBI liaison officer proclaimed, after a long silence.

"Go ahead, Amaan," he directed. "Give your statement. I'll wait right here."

The officer's eyes swung at me. "Mr Singh, shall we?" My pink eye, seemingly, pared down his strict intentions. "Please," he said as he slid the tissue box closer to me.

"A man in a Yankees baseball hat flew out of nowhere and threatened me with a gun," I said.

"Sorry, Mr Singh," the officer interrupted. "We need to know from the beginning."

"It's a bit blurry," I replied. "It was a rather unusual flight."

"We can do this tomorrow morning," he said, evoking a strict no from Veer.

"Okay. I'll try." I said, wiping my nose with the tissue. Insult was okay. Reliving the insult repeatedly wasn't. "I boarded the plane. We were in the air for less than an hour when the air hostess interrupted me with her comments."

"What were her comments?"

"She said, 'Sir, I have to tell you that no one went into the bathroom after you and the alarm is broken'."

"So she suspected you broke the toilet alarm."

"Or dreamed," I mocked. *I shouldn't have.*

"What happened next?" he asked, conveniently turning deaf to my tone.

"She just melted on the ground."

"Melted?"

"She fainted. Everyone thought she was dead."

"Then what happened?"

"I stood up to help her as I'm a medical student, then the man in Yankee cap attacked me."

"Do you have any idea why he attacked you?"

"Yes. He later identified himself as an air marshal."

"And then what did you do, when you got to know that?"

"I offered him to see my ID."

"And did he look at your ID?"

"Yes, he did. After minutes of deliberation, he allowed me to resuscitate the steward, and she survived."

"And this is how you guys reward a good citizen?" My brother interrupted, hammering the liaison officer in a strange cold way.

"Sir, the incident caused great disruption for over three hundred passengers, not just your brother."

"But he was the one knuckled down and assaulted," Veer countered his argument.That made the liaison officer roll and pack his tongue back.

"I'll see you at the palace, Amaan," Veer pronounced, after the interview with the FBI. I couldn't tell if he was happy, mad, or just disappointed. I wished I wasn't a burden on him, and that's exactly what I had become.

In the thick darkness, the limo swiftly rowed through the outskirts of Delhi. The monsoon had lost all its shame. As if flooded canyons weren't enough, a man couldn't even see his own arms in this fog.

"Sir, what have you brought with you?" The turbaned limo driver chuckled, baiting me for small talk, which I was in no mood for. I had no stamina to smile, but I still smiled. I think it came out all wrong, though. I was still perplexed by the bizarreness of the choking steward.

What the hell happened on that plane? I remember the turbulence, I remember the steward, I remember saving her, but I couldn't remember hurting her. *Did I really hurt her?* The spikes of that possibility stabbed my conscience. *It had to be a coincidence. A strange one.* Not just any strange, a paranormal strange one. That's it. That's what it was – a paranormally strange event.

In my mind, the debate was still thriving when my eyes turned onto the fogged window. Gushes of rain splashed on it, only to scatter the fog into neatly printed passage of my mother's repeated advice. *"Stay close to Veer. He'll protect you."* I panicked, throwing myself on the other side of the seat, my face hiding into my hands, my eyes shut under it.

Slowly, I plucked the fingers away and my mother's face flashed, then the window wiped clean of the words, and her face. Before I could gather my wits, the limo jerked to a stop, right at the imperial staircase of the palace.

Saira

"Baida uncle, where is your moustache?" I inquired in the Cutten Bazaar, the thriving downtown of Attanooga. Nothing had changed here in the last ten years, except for Baida uncle's moustache.

My eyes were drawn into a panoramic look around the Victorian-era town, with the grey cobblestone roads under my feet, street fairs upfront, and giant apple-shaped balloons tied to the copper lampposts, and rolling wood tires under tan brown horseback carts.

A smile tattooed, unlike just a few hours ago on my way here when I hadn't winked even for a second for the whole two hours. Not when I saw distinctive bronze bell atop my mother's house at the foot of those hills.

This was my declaration of war with my fear. There was no stopping me from doing my own show. I earned it.

"Oh, is that you, Saira?" My presence had electrified the rather settled persona that Baida uncle was. "It is you." He snooped through his low nose glasses, carefully looking at me. "Look at you; you're so much more beautiful now."

I felt good. I felt fresh, unlike the last couple of months where even in my dreams I no longer had pink cheeks. The body wasn't slim, nice silky brown hair seemed burned in coal, and my light brown eyes sculpted in dark circles. I thought the breakup from Neil would make me feel only good, but nope. Whenever I felt elated for dumping him, I also felt the grip of loneliness tightening its noose, suffocating me to depression.

"How is your mother?" he asked.

"She's fine, uncle," I sputtered. I'd have reacted the same way if he had asked about the stray dog loitering the street in front of me. *Hate is purer than love. There's no place for adulterants.*

"Let's talk about you, uncle." I had to maneuver to get back to business.

He smiled as if he knew I was fishing for something else. "What's there to talk about me, Saira? You're the celebrity of Attanooga."

"Celebrity?"

"Your mother never fails to mention all the culprits you have put behind bars in that show of yours." His frail voice breached into a cough. "Your mother is proud of you, and we are all proud of you, too."

"Thank you, Baida uncle. And, I have breaking news for you." His arousing curiosity was the tuna to net him in my trap. "I am going to host my own show!"

"That's great news." His eyes lit up. "So your mother keeps the big news all to herself."

It felt like a sharp sting of radiation on a non-cancerous cell. Once destroyed, nothing healthy could grow in it, and nothing did for ten short years. It had worked well, until now, of course.

"I was thinking it's time for you to come on TV." I kept the smile on my face.

"Me? No no... I'm too old for that." His harried voice cracked further.

"What old? Even Amitabh Bachchan is on TV at this age. And you're younger!"

"What will I do on TV?"

"Uncle, I'm thinking of doing a special on Queen Sana. And I want to start here at Cutten Bazaar with you." He looked at me for a few moments before realizing what I had said.

"Saira, we're small people."

"And we live in a democracy, where the people have the power, the voice."

"Did you talk to His Highness?" My mother's age-old tale of cautionary words about the town and its loyalty to the royals bounced off my metals. However, I stayed quiet.

"You see this street, Saira? What's different about this than any other part of our country?"

"It's very pretty!" I exclaimed.

He smiled. He was old and wise. I think he knew exactly how to cut through my bullshit, but he pretended otherwise. "The street has no electric wires." The monotony of his tone was powerful, in a unique way. "In 1952, His Highness' father reconstructed this entire downtown and then gave it to us for free, because a friend of his from England had said,'I have to fold the curtain of wires and poverty just to see my own face in the mirror'."

"We are what we are because of His Highness and his family, Saira, and that's why no one will be willing to talk to you. I, as the president of Attanooga Shopper's Association, can't permit them to."

I could feel the carpet pulled from right under by feet. I was falling headfirst on my own words, and they were about to hit me hard.

Amaan

"You have to do one thing for me, Amaan," Veer had suggested after the plane fiasco. He wasn't the one to let go of his favours or to refrigerate them for later use. He wanted to roast them fresh right off the butcher shop.

"You don't have to ask, brother." I was elated to be of help.

"I need you to be the face of a campaign."

"Which campaign?"

"You'll know soon," he said. "For now, I'd like you to sit in a meeting for me."

"Sure." I had my questions, but I was also too eager to please. Anything that could stifle the faintest inquiry into what happened on the plane, because, the pebbles of that event weren't quite in order inside my head, too. "Just tell me the time and place."

His smiled and the way he looked, calmed me. "New Delhi tomorrow. Wouldn't you ask what the meeting is about?"

"Does it matter?"

"But you should know," he had insisted. "We're selling our palace."

He waited for me to react. "Great." That's all I had said.

"Very well then." He had patted on my back. "It's good to have you here brother."

"And one more thing," Veer had expanded. "Can you promise me that you'll stay away from that trashy cottage?"

I didn't care about the palace. However, forbiddance from the cottage felt strange. That was my own solace. Perhaps I had sinned and the reprimand was correct. I must concede. "I promise, brother."

I drove past the cottage hill on my way to Delhi. It looked like a bear hiding on the hill. A strange feeling of a forbidden goodbye lingered. I snapped away. *Goodbye, cottage*.

Therefore, here I was scorching to death in the name of selling the namesake palace which I thought would be simple; money changes hands and all done. Nope, it rarely worked that way.

"The liability clause here is unacceptable to us. It should say 'we will not' instead of 'we shall not'."

Lawyers are rare species who have to justify their presence and high dollars, and how do they do it, by fixing the tenses in a sentence.

"I want to make sure we make best use of Mr Singh's time." A petite figure flamed up. *Where was she hiding until now?* "We can prepare some clarification points offline. We can then discuss with you, sir." She pointed straight at me, her eyes chirped like a pair of beautiful red birds, her smile hiding under her nude lips. I liked the attention, though I wasn't sure if I was worth it.

"Ah, sure." I grappled with words. "I can sit, but it'll be helpful if you can coach me the legalities in plain English."

"Absolutely." She stood no taller than Natalie Portman did, but the fumes of her fire had already spread. She sashayed from one end of the conference room to another; her eyes looking up into the sky, her face lounged in the unspoken awe, her gliding steps electrifying the wires of every dull head in the room. Pretending to look away was futile.

"Better now?" She settled in an empty seat next to me, and all the lusty eyes quickly rolled off the cliff and back into their books.

"I didn't catch your name?" I questioned.

"Ria." She creased her cheeks through a lively smile.

That's where the conversation between her and I stopped, and the room quickly shackled back into the words of black suits and red ties. That was until a ding-dong beep.

"Sorry, I tried to help you!:) (Sic)" the message popped up on my computer.

I had forgotten that we were also on Skype, in conference with other lawyers of the same firm. *How many lawyers did we really need to fix this contract? Who cares!* At least now, I had my out.

"I am still fenced, bruised, and dying a slow death," I replied.

"Lol. (Sic)"

"Where were you hiding?"

"Behind my old fat boss!"

"Was that on purpose?"

"No. He gains weight by second. He has already gained a dozen doughnuts in the last hour alone, enough to hide me behind it."

This was the first time in months that I didn't feel the crane of remorse pulling me from under the ground. I felt at ground, feeling every grain of air going in, seeing every fume of toxicity coming out of me.

"So, you live in Delhi?"

"I do. Born and raised here! 100% Delhi girl!"

"Show me then."

"Show you what?"

"Show me around Delhi, babe. Can't dare to ask for anything more."

"You better not!"

The chat paused. I was certain it was my doing. I had a knack of messing up small talks. I had a knack of messing up. Period.

"Lol. (Sic)" She came back to life with laughter, and the smileys rolled again. I think they were laughing.

"Ooh. I am in trouble already."

"Big one."

"How can I get out of it?"

"You can't. You need to be punished."

"That sounds scary."

"It is."

"Is this how you punish all your clients?"

"Only the naughty ones."

We were two lost souls in a world of fat, oily people whose only talent was that they had a thesaurus on their computers. We were lost for full eight hours, and after that, and they all wanted to have dinner together as well. *What the hell?*

"So which place should we burn down?" I asked her in the hotel lobby.

"My boss is going to kill me," she simpered through her soft lips. That's all I could see. Every word came with a shudder.

"Why? Because you're so beautiful?" I felt she hated me moving so fast.

"Don't flatter me," she teased.

A crumb of courage slithered. I turned and looked her in the eyes. It felt as if I didn't disgust her, after all. Instead, kindness floated in them.

She continued, "Because I'm skipping dinner."

"What are you doing?" she entreated as my phone bubbled up a dial tone.

"Hello Mr Kapur, this is Amaan," I announced.

She froze in the moment. Her arms weren't moving. Her mouth gaped, even her tongue froze.

"How about we do the dinner tomorrow?" I turned the topic out.

"Absolutely, Mr Singh," he replied instantly. "As you wish."

She thawed once the call ended. A smile woke up her pink cheeks.

"So, tell me what are we doing to 'live Delhi' today?" I asked.

"It depends on what you like." She smiled gently.

"*Hip-hop* music, *angrezi* liquor, and meat *ka nivala.*"

"I'd never have taken you for a hip-hop fan." She blushed.

I must have twitched a happy nerve with the whole hip-hop talk. This was good! I was getting right back on track.

She mulled for a while. Murmuring different names, and then crossing them out even before they sparked. She cleared her throat, and that's when I knew we had a winner. "Why don't we go to the house party? And we can grab your chicken and lamb, or like you call meat ka nivala on the way?"

I had once again outdone my awkwardness. I just did the whole gangster knuckle shake only to find her fingers entangled somewhere between my silliness and her embarrassment.

"I'm not a real gangster." I was chuckling, smiling, laughing; whatever it took to find my way out of awkwardness.

"I think I know that." She painted a familiar smile. The one I had suddenly grown addicted to.

It was 1 a.m., and this was no ordinary house party. The cracking floor of this place lay evidence that the dance warriors of Delhi weren't to be messed with. I could feel the vibe; this one had thirsty teeth, lots of it.

"Whose house is this?" I whispered into her ear.

"Why does it matter?" She pulled me onto the floor, turned around, my arms locked to hers, skidding down until they rested above her hips.

"This is the real deal." My lips touched her ears, and a wild sensation shook me down the spine.

She turned, looked up, signalling me to stoop.

"Because this is," she reaffirmed.

I got what she was saying. This wasn't really a house party; it was 'the' house party, a theme club!

"How amazing!" I said.

"Come dance now," she whispered, slowly carting me through the crowd, swaying through the jazzed resonance of ethnic *dhol* beats, until we had become part of the crowd, with me crumbling the floor with my foot thumps and she raising the temperature with her sweat-less body.

Hours must have passed; it felt as much, until we sprinkled out of the spell when the music grinded to a screeching halt.

"Now is the time for speed dating, oops?" the DJ announced.

The crowd howled to complete his sentence, "Speed dancing!"

"Don't go too far," Ria purred.

"What is this?" I asked.

"You'll get to know." Her words cued up to the music barraging through the speaker, then came the army of boots and sandals bruising the cedar planks beneath. The rumblings of the floor swayed in the violence of music, and the twisted theme of flipping partners sparked a creature with a thousand heads. I was floating stateless, grinding, dirty dancing, gliding to a new partner, then again to a new one, and again, until I was thrown to a different girl.

She looks familiar, very familiar. I couldn't place her just yet. The ecstasy had blocked my brain, and I didn't mind that, at all. We swung around, slithering on each other's skin, drunken by the alcohol. This moment was something else. Her face sprinkled in her sweet sweat and the way she looked at me, I knew she felt the same! We didn't speak a word to each other, and then the music changed. I drifted away from her and back in the arms of my sweet Ria.

"I'll be back in a second," Ria whispered.

Saira

Six showers and four dresses later, I could still feel Neil on me. My temples raged with heat, my eyes quenched with pain, and my body broke with chills.

"Where are you? It's been an hour," I texted Neil again. If he were here, I'd punch him. I know he read it the moment he got the message. My eyes glued to the message screen, hunting for those grey dots to appear, but nothing thus far. What a letdown. *Is this how he thinks he will continue to lap me under his thighs?* We had a deal and now he was breaking it.

"Hello, beautiful." The faraway tone of Neil's words from behind me made me sick. My arms were out, my fists formed, but then I had to drink my own kool-aid. *Today he lives.*

"You're late," I sassed.

"I'm sorry." He was suddenly on his feet, perhaps thinking of a way to pacify me. "But I'm positive that the rewards would be worth the wait."

"What reward?"

"You'll see."

"Alright, Neil!" I had to set my bar. "In all these years you still don't know what I like and what I don't."

"It's not like that," he slurred. "Calm down."

Why is he such a smug? "Oh, the suspense!" I grated.

"You know how I do it."

He had to learn when to draw a line between reality and fiction, but this wasn't my problem to fix. "WHAT are we DOING here?" I was firm.

His fun attitude suddenly whitewashed. He thought he did not know how I could work him up, poor bastard.

"The first rule of a reality-based program is that you have to choose the right players." His preachy mode was depressing, but in all candidness, I needed a bit of it, especially after the Cutten Bazaar fiasco.

He continued. "And, you don't have to wait for the right moment to meet the players. You create or adapt to existing opportunities."

"Can we come straight to the point?"

"When you called me a week back for help, you know what the first thing I did was?"

"I don't know." I couldn't even pretend to be interested.

"Spin a guess."

"Dreamt of me in some erotic way." I was clueless as to why I was feeding his fantasy for dirty talk.

"Yes. But I also engaged my private detective firm on all members of the Royal family."

That was a great idea. "I should do the same!" I submitted.

"Nah. I got it covered," he assured. "See? Veer is out of town and Amaan is in," he dragged for his theatrical effect. "New Delhi!"

"How did you like my investigation?" He enunciated every syllable obnoxiously.

"It's good." I kept my placidity right where it was before the conversation, at least on the outside.

"Now you got to find a way to introduce yourself to him."

"I'd rather not use your sex bait tactic here," I surmised, hiding the storm within.

"We all use people for what we need." His lowbrow look was good enough a reason to punch him in his face, but I refrained. I had to find a way to get in Attanooga, and it couldn't be Amaan.

"Alright, let's dance," he offered.

"Are you going to carry that flowery drink to the floor?"

"Oh. I'm sorry."

"Shall we?" His arms poised to take me to the floor, only I wanted to damage them, but I couldn't. "And I have a surprise after the dance that you won't regret." His curious words defeated my repulsion for him. *I had to find a way to jumpstart my series.*

The ocean had spilled onto the floor. The spell had begun. The tradition to swap dance partners on the floor in this fancy club called The House Party, and here I was swirling away, until a familiar smell took control of my reigns, pulling me in, moving our bodies in rhythm, body to body, his broad hard chest, my back; his long lean legs, my hips. *I need to stop. No, I don't, I want to, I don't want to, I want to break free. I want to be glued here, forever.*

He was drifting away. I felt cold down to my bones; I needed his cover. I looked at him in frenzy, his face swimming above the mist, and in that moment, our eyes strung together, refusing to look past. It was he. *It was Amaan.*

I turned away to Neil, only if it was to cover. I had to turn away from Amaan. I had to turn away from my past, a past so blue that I couldn't see it clearly.

"Saira, is that you?" Ria trilled out of nowhere. "What are you doing here?"

This was the last thing I wanted tonight – a college pageantry rivalry.

"Dancing, I guess!"

"Can I ask you a favour?" Her tone was as pretentious as she was. "Would you mind not dancing again with my company?" There you go; she didn't even wait for me to respond. It wasn't as if I didn't have enough reasons to be raging today that I needed this one, too.

"Sure." I turned away.

I didn't even know who her man was. I didn't care.

"Hi, Ria!" echoed the familiar voice that once had innocence and still did, only it was heavier now. I had to walk away.

"Are you Amaan Singh? Attanooga?" Neil appeared out of nowhere, thwarting my attempt to escape.

"Yes, I am," he replied.

"Saira, do you know Amaan?" Neil's question meant that I had to turn, and I did, dragging my feet, hoping that a miracle would annihilate this moment.

"Hello!" I was reluctant. The only pleasure I got was to rub it in Ria's face.

I could feel Amaan's eyes digging into my face. "I knew you looked familiar, but your voice, it's still the same." His eyes lit up with joy. "Saira, the mocking jay Saira?"

I swung, collar to chin, and he pulled me right into his arms, covering me just the way Ria would have never wanted it. Ria didn't have to speak, but she did anyway. "Looks like we all know each other."

"We know each other," Ria and I really spoke on top of each other. I was beginning to hate me now, too. The only way I could have stayed longer was if Ria died, paralyzed, or if someone threw a drink onto her, or anything to humiliate her.

"I got to go. You guys have fun," I retorted.

Ria's pretentious smile had drained the last of my happy blood; all that was remaining was charred black fluid of rage.

"Where? Let me get a round of drinks," Neil interjected.

Drinks. Really? We're ready to pound flesh off each other and you want me to have vodka and cranberry with her?

"I have a story to finish," I rebuffed.

"She does all these purse camera exposé," Ria whispered into Amaan's ears, but I could clearly hear it, and I was sure so did several others around us. *This girl is so fake.* I really wanted to spit back at her, but I behaved.

"She's moved up." Neil for once said something that made me feel nice.

"Congratulations," Amaan praised, drawing no reaction on his calm face. I could never tell how he felt. He always had this poker face. "What have you moved up to?" he asked.

"I'm getting my own show," I announced.

"That's amazing," Amaan lauded, trying to tear up the awkwardness of us meeting after a decade.

Bundles of silent nervous moments were broken when Ria opened her filthy mouth. "We'll see you guys around then."

"Always a pleasure meeting you, Ria." Gosh, I had to kiss her goodbye.

"We should have a chat." Neil's objective was darted, and even though this was to help me, I wished this moment just swept away. Amaan in flesh didn't come alone. He was unleashing thousands of foot soldiers of the past, and they all had sharp knives.

Amaan

I didn't believe in coincidences, until today. My skin swelled with excitement. For ten years, she had been a ghost, completely untraceable.

"I'll see you around then?" I asked.

She smiled and vamoosed. I had many questions to ask, but she turned me away. In an instance, her sense of discard had come rushing back to me.

"Small world, huh!" Ria conceded with her ever-lively smile.

"Yup. But let's continue our moment."

"Are you sure?" she queried, waiting for me to pull her closer, and I did. The warmth of her heart infused a comfort that I had longed for months.

"I absolutely am!" This time, I didn't whisper into her ear. I whispered through my lips onto hers. She swam along for a bit, pulled out and sprayed a look riddled in cryptic messages.

The next time, I got hold of my senses. I was still on the floor, my knuckles had cracked, half of my knee had dissolved, and I could hear my heartbeat through my tongue. *Her wish to dance attacked me, and boy, did she make me dance!* Now it was my turn to command. She wasn't standing on her legs anymore. She was in my arms, her heart snuggled to mine, her lips smudged with mine, and us breathing into each other.

Saira

"Thank you for coming here, ladies and gentlemen." Veer, the king of a dethroned kingdom had taken over the stage and snatched the chatter straight off the football stadium-size audience. Even a chair didn't dare move.

"We've been a close knit community for at least two centuries. We never gave up on our loyalty. We never gave up on our culture. We never gave up on our people. Today, we honour the citizens of Attanooga who have helped maintain the soul of this town, the charm of this town, the pride of this town."

The crowd erupted with firebrand chants of, "Guard us, our queen. Attanooga has lost its sheen."

My cameras were furiously rolling, recording the fetish for loss of their queen.

"I'm indebted to have a family like you." Veer notched up the decibel, spraying silence all over the arena. "She's still with us!" he declared to a cheering crowd, "To guide us. And in her honour, we'll rebuild our town and our employment!" The crowd rejoiced with an over-brimmed hubris.

"Snow isn't the only thing that brings tourists to our town… it's you! The people, the spirit, the food and our unique culture."

He paused to a buzzing dance of hands. "I wanted to bring this big surprise later, but I can't control my excitement, so here it is. We will have a world class hotel in Attanooga, by Taj group!" The applause thundered in a thick smoke of pride.

"The people of Attanooga don't have to leave their homes and parents. We'll bring world-class economy to our town." The crowd applauded. "And then every town of our state will be modelled after Attanooga, and, what is our goal?"

True to his showman style, what he was to reveal didn't unveil through words. Firecrackers from all directions mercilessly stabbed the sky, etching the cloud with glowing designs. When it all ended, the sky shone with the new slogan of Attanooga, *Shinier with you*.

The vigor of the crowd spilled through their teeth. "Shinier with you. Shinier with you..." The chanting grew louder and louder, and I had a feeling that it wasn't going to stop anytime soon.

"And, I'd like to re-introduce to you, your prince and my kid brother Amaan, who will lead this effort for Attanooga!"

"This is a beautiful shot, ma'am," my camera operator pronounced. Without any thought, I quickly pounced on the peddle and drilled my eyes, only to find me staring right at Amaan, with the camera dancing in lock steps to Amaan's.

He had changed a lot. Last night in the club was a bit blurry, but here it was clear as a diamond. Then along came Pison, taunting me with crawls under by veins, yapping. "This is your ticket in the royal family, you dumb girl. He's your perfect bait, look at his ignorance, so paramount. You're going to trap him, or else you'll be trapped in my slimy stings."

Amaan

"Good morning, Amaan." The morning sun erected a white pyramid on Ria. Her cheeks dug rosier, lips printed redder.

"What time is it?" I asked, trying to visor the sun from my eyes.

"It's 11 a.m." Ria sparkled.

She looked much fuller than last night. I tried to snap away, but was apprehended red-handed with my eyes still dug in her.

"You're aging backwards," I muttered away from the embarrassment.

"It's okay," she said. "You don't have to feel guilty about last night. We're two consenting adults."

I pretended to look around her bedroom as if hunting to draw out the coffee smell.

"Do I smell eggs?" I snickered, hoping I'd landslide my awkwardness under it.

She stood, puppeteering me through her arms until we were out of her bedroom and onto her mahogany kitchen table decorated with fresh cut pineapples, a sunny side egg reposed on a seven-grain toast, and a bowl of coffee piping fresh from the hot spring.

"Wow!" I exclaimed.

"I have to go. I'm late already." She gently forked her fingers through my hair, rubbing away the splitting headache from last night.

I held her hand. "Come here," I simpered, pulling her into my arms, and she fell willingly. I didn't say much. We just snuggled, listening to each other's heart, wrapped in a thick ball of cotton.

"I really do have to go," she implored.

"Can't you just skip work?"

"I'm working on your hotel deal, and I need to be there to make sure your family, and you," she planted a misty kiss next to my lips, "are protected."

"Why fuss so much? It's just a hotel deal."

She stayed mum, but her probing eyes were noticeable. "It's for you." She quickly snapped back to the topic. "And tomorrow I have to be in Mumbai to go through a due diligence workshop."

"Wait. Mumbai?"

"It's just a day. I'll be back tomorrow."

"What due diligence?"

"It's something my father wants me to do."

"But then what about the Attanooga event?"

"Is this the yearly town hall celebration event?" she quizzed. "I totally missed that," she said soon thereafter. "But. Come here. You will be fine. It's your event. Your family's. There'll be plenty of familiarity."

"I'm not going alone." I grumbled. "The last time I went to that event, I was sixteen. Familiarity is a strong word to describe my affinity to the gala's crowd."

"Just this one time, please?" she adjured.

What in the world happened to me? I thought. I barely knew her and my heart was freezing to death at the first cradle of separation. "We'll see each other tomorrow then?" I asked.

"Sure, I'd like that," she purred softly.

"Can I drop you to the airport?"

"I'm not going to the airport."

"I'm not going to allow you to take a train."

"I'm not." She smiled.

"You have a private jet? Don't you?"

"I'll see you." She saddled a kiss in the air.

My heart squeezed until the gullet squeaked.

"It takes you to a past life, that was so serene, doesn't it, Amaan?" The curious thought, and the voice, was as comforting as the warmth from the orange embers in Attanooga's oldest and most extravagant clubroom.

"Interesting way to put it!" I professed to the beautiful face, the one I had seen not too long ago, but it was a first for this evening.

"You hear the silence of this town?" she asked. "It's like everyone has receded under blankets, resting in peace because they have you and your brother watching their back."

"I'd trade this snooze-filled afterparty for a good night sleep any day!" Her lips carved her face into a happy smile.

"You haven't changed, Saira. Not at all." Our hands reached over the orange embers in one of the hundreds stone fire pits around us.

"You too. Still the popular guy." She smiled to the fire. "All eyes are on you now." She turned to me, reeking of mischief.

"Oh, well."

"The torchbearer to memorialize the legacy of our beloved queen of Attanooga." She re-declared my newly-minted responsibility, courtesy my brother.

"This is called woman power." Saira stood taller with her words. "The abandonment only swelled her popularity."

"She didn't really abandon Attanooga," I rebuffed.

"Of course not. I don't mean it in a bad way," Saira clarified.

"No. I get it." I felt a pinch of relief. In my mother's taking care of me, her odd child, she ended up vanishing from this town. "She never really stopped caring, you know. She balanced."

Saira stayed quiet, only to whisper, "A lot has happened in these last ten years."

"I know." Our eyes weren't very honest.

"Where is Ria?" Saira quickly turned the page.

"She's in Mumbai. Can't miss her dad's wish."

"You are a lucky man. Congratulations!"

"Thank you." It was a pleasant change, the one that sketched a smile on my face. "Do you guys know each other?" I asked.

"Yup." She smiled. "Lady Shri Ram College."

"Ah. Then I can get all the juicy details about her?"

"You wish. I don't think I'm going to break the gal-pal bond." Her mischief pounced from under her furry paws.

"Is that what you girls were talking about last night? In the club, I saw you and Ria whisper into each other's ears."

"Well…" She jazzed her eyes. "That was…" she paused.

"This suspense has my entire breath hostage."

"Sorry. If I tell you, I'll have to kill you," she teased.

"Oh, c'mon! You always do that." All at once, I felt we were back where we had left a decade ago. I could smell her the same way I did back then.

"How long have you guys been dating?" she quipped.

"We're getting to know each other."

"I know that line." Her smile spilled her cheeks like a Scabiosa flower. "C'mon, she's perfect for you."

"How? Why?"

"Why not! She's royal-ish with all the new money."

"I don't care about any of that."

"I know, but it has shaped her into this pretty, not-too-petite dame! Just the way you like it."

"Whatever. What are you doing here anyway?" I had to change that topic.

"Plans change. Some because of good reasons and some because of bad ones."

"Let's start with the good one." I was intrigued.

"I'm stalking you."

"It all makes sense now. Why didn't I think of it before? Where's my lawyer? Wait, that's Ria!"

"I don't think that's going to help you at all."

"I'm in trouble then, huh?"

"Big trouble."

"If the good reason is that bad, I'm not sure if I really want to know the bad one for your presence here."

"Some things are unavoidable," she yapped, and then I heard another familiar voice climbing atop my shoulders.

"My dear Amaan!" This one I knew instantly.

"Hello, Mrs Gaina." I turned, only to bump into a timeless abundance of beauty. "Congratulations on your award!"

"Thank you," she whispered in glee, only to wipe it off a moment later. "I am so sorry for your loss." She swallowed me in her heart-weeping hug.

"Look at you, all tall and handsome like your father." Her smile didn't do a good job of hiding her tears.

"Looks like you two found each other!" Mrs Gaina turned to Saira.

"Yes, we did, Mommy." Saira was reluctant.

"She came all the way from Delhi to see me get this humanitarian award by your brother," Mrs Gaina spoke with pride.

"That's right." Saira upbraided her claim. "Bad reason!"

"She hasn't been to this town for almost as much as you, Amaan," Mrs Gaina said.

It took a moment for her words to sink in, and then it dawned; and along came a foggy "Why?"

Strangely tucked in a hay of pleasantry; the camping in the forest, Saira and I in our pajamas, zipped in an airtight tent, flaming our eyes through the candle, playing 'invite the ghost', sleeping with her dog, Pillow.

"Thanks for the tell-all, Mommy." One didn't need a fortuneteller to measure Saira's condescending tone.

I could see that inch-and-a-half wrinkle of discomfort on Mrs Gaina caused by Saira's blunt reply. She turned to me, her hands around my face. "I am so sorry for your loss again, my boy."

"You know it's hard to keep loved ones close when they're with you; and it's harder to let them go when gone." She turned to Saira's disdain look, only to return her eyes back to me.

"Oh, well. First we need to clearly demark both of you with a tattoo or something. I get confused sometimes, whether Saira and you are twin sisters," I turned the topic.

"Oh, you silly boy," Mrs Gaina smiled, quite in contrast to Saira, whose mood had further valleyed down an anger cliff.

"No, I'm serious and quite honestly, not even twins. You could actually be confused with her younger sister," I said.

"Oh, this is too much," she replied.

"I'm sure Saira gets that a lot." Saira's reaction was nothing more than her cold breath.

"Oh well, it's time for me to go now." Mrs Gaina bid goodbye.

"You want to box?" I stole the opportunity. Didn't even give Saira a chance to walk away, which she was all but ready to do.

"Sure," she said. "But I get to hit you first." The way she looked, I was certain she had already bloodied me.

"All that fury," I grumbled. "I meant box ball dance."

She didn't move a thread in her body, not even her brows.

"Sorry for the disappointment," I said.

Finally, the windshield of her anger cracked a smile. Just a tiny one. Enough for me to take her in my wings.

"What are you doing?" she asked, paralyzed by my quick actions, and like two well-designed snowflakes, we landed on the outdoor dance floor nestled in the hills, her nestled in my arms.

"Oh, I don't know this. I'm not much of a formal dancer." She began babbling, now that all eyes were on us.

"Let's tune for our prince on the floor," the orchestra maestro announced, drumming one beat for every hill surrounding us.

"I know you got your moves. Come, let's do it."

"I can't. I'm too shy. I have to go."

"This is your last chance, or else for the rest of the dance, you're going to be spinning, not on the floor, but in my lap."

As the complex rhythm of violin weaved the fabric of symphony, her slippery steps slithered like a pro, just like we had planned to do ten years ago, the night of my birthday.

"Feeling better now?" I asked.

"No." She smiled, dispensing an erotic citrus smell.

"You still use the same perfume?"

"I don't use perfume."

"How can you naturally smell so exotic then?" I made sure I didn't mix my *x* with my *r*.

"Are you flirting with me?" Her smile poured mischief. "Ria and I are friends. I'm never going to betray her."

"Slow down, beautiful. A man can't talk lightly with his ex-girlfriend?"

"That was ten years ago. We were kids."

"We're not kids anymore."

"Exactly."

"In that case, you have a lot to answer for."

"What?" She seemed innocently surprised like there was nothing out of ordinary. "Grow up!"

"I will. Once we sit down and talk it through."

"Don't tell me you're not over me yet?"

"I'm so over you. But that doesn't stop me from talking to you about our missed time, does it?"

"On one condition."

"Don't ask me to slit my throat."

"I'll save that for later."

"Then anything for you."

"We'll talk about it later."

"Later when?" I asked.

The caffeinated strings of violin came to a gentle stop. The drums stopped marching. The song had ended.

"Mesmerizing," bawled the maestro, trickling a waterfall of claps.

A messenger whispered into my ears, "His Highness would like you to meet the Scindia family and Rampur Royals."

"So? Any decision?" I asked Saira before leaving.

In her response, she chose to stare, and stare and stare.

Saira

"Get me a cabernet, please." I politely recused back to my master plan, away from the beady eyes of the overzealous waiter in the Attanooga's clubroom restaurant.

Thirty-six hours since the last meeting with Amaan, here I was, ready to trap him in my net. "Careful was the word," Pison had said. "Strap it to your necklace."

"You have to turn a soldier into your spy."

The storyboard of the first scene looped in my head. The opening shot that would humanize the royalty in Amaan. Casual/Fun prince, not knowing that he was soon to be stabbed by the darkness of his mother's death. I longed to grieve for him, but not today. Pixels of infidelity were yet to be added. After all, the price I paid to get this far was neither recoverable nor forgivable.

The Pison in me laughed, stinging hard, "Oh poor Saira. You have nothing to give but your body. That too, to Neil?" Her nauseating laughter bled my ears.

A slushy voice galvanized me back to the spoons and knives. "Ma'am, everything okay?" the waiter asked.

"Yes," came an instant reply from me. That didn't stop the waiter from staring at my fist, shaped like a knuckleball, wrestling with the tablecloth.

I repeated, "Yes. Everything is fine." My hands receded onto my handbag, the smile uncaged. The chatter in the room grew back its locks. The Pison was still around, and so was her cynical throbbing.

The clock ticked thirty minutes past noon, the time Amaan had promised to be here.

Pison hissed with her antlers, "This is why guys think you are easy. Make a rule to stroll in late, like what Ria does. That's what gets their attention."

Maybe this repulsive creature was right. I stood, my hands fidgeted down the purse, ready to turn off my little spy cam, then for one last time I looked at the entrance, hoping he might dash in. But nope. All my hopes were shattered.

"Looking for someone?" Just then, a voice from the back drizzled. It was him.

I liked when I was alone in my office cabin; eating take out dinner by myself, drinking cabernet in a pomegranate juice bottle. *Why hasn't Amaan called me? Did I rub him the wrong way?*

"Ready for our meeting with Suri?" Neil asked in his quintessential sarcasm. While I tried not to answer his every question, his prerogative was quite the opposite, snooping around everything that lay in my brand new office.

"What is this?" He gasped.

"I think you know well, that's the storyboard for the series." However, that didn't thaw his dramatic gasp. "This is from Queen Sana's point of view," I continued.

"Is this for History channel?" The ice frost on his mouth finally melted.

"What do you mean?"

"Do you know what our channel's brand is?" I could feel the ruckus congregate in the air around us. "Oh, dear Saira, we make horseshit look like a fucking mysterious blob from aliens." He paused. "You heard Suri, right? He wants a decent show."

"Suri may want a lot of things, but decent ain't one of them." I was about to throw up a volcano the moment I realized what Neil had made me do. I wanted to bloody his nose for trapping me to barf against Suri. But I had to let it go; we were already late for the meeting.

"What do you have for us, Saira?" Suri was excited, which was about to be crushed by Neil.

Suri remained quiet throughout the presentation, which wasn't a good sign. I could feel him in my head, walking all over my thoughts. Saying, *this is wrong; this doesn't belong here; throw this one out*. The writing was on the wall. *This is pathetic.*

"Oh well," Neil taunted. "This is a really good start," he paused, signaling that an act change was on the cards. "Let's work a bit more." He quite mercilessly stressed the words just a tiny-tooney bit, "To get a good three-act story out there." He paused again, making the dirt road clear for my words.

"Neil, how would you structure this story?" Suri asked.

"I can start..." I interjected right away. *I'll not allow Neil to speak out of his ill mouth, not anymore.* "We can start with the romance of Queen Sana and His Highness Rudra Singh, and then we talk about the murder and how it created a rift between the two, then her going away to US to take care of her son, and then her final days."

Neil smoothly paved his way in. "I like the first act. I also like the third act."

"Thank you!" I bleated. Well knowing that his degenerate ideas could be up next.

"I think we can add some flavour to the second, though." He paused before throttling his venom sting again. The next few minutes felt like I was being water-boarded with sick fantasies of this frustrated idiot. One after the other, the statement stung every breathing cell in my brain, knocking them all out.

Finally, it was over. There was a pause, and Suri turned to me. "What do you think?"

I wanted to excuse myself for a second, just enough to pulp Neil into the ground. "That's a nice touch of fiction there," I said instead.

"You are going to find that out, right? Whether it's fiction or fact," Suri said.

I couldn't believe he didn't choke Neil's sick idea right away. What a shame! I thought he would be different, but no! All men are the same, sick to the gut.

"Okay." I was non-conformant.

"At least this gives you a framework to work up your interviews with the royal family members." Suri paused. "Speaking of royal family, did we make any headway?"

"Yes, we did," I replied instantly. Even I liked my confidence when I said that. "I had lunch with Amaan, and he liked the idea."

"You know him by first name?"

"Yes. I went to school with him."

Suri's confidence rose. "That's excellent. When is the first interview then?"

"Soon," I assured.

"We have four weeks to wrap this. That means we should have started this four weeks ago, too. There ain't a whole lot of time," he clarified calmly.

"I get it," I reassured. "I'll call him tonight."

Amaan

"So, today I got a surprise visitor." Ria's declaration sent my heart in an antsy. A quiet evening in her penthouse was about to get noisy.

"Is that an ex-boyfriend of yours?"

"No, silly." She rubbed her hands on mine, and suddenly the explosions in my head iced. I could once again hear the soft crackle of the fire. "It was your ex-girlfriend, Saira," she replied.

"Saira, my ex?" I chuckled. "I didn't remember that part. Maybe I missed a memo."

"Well. She remembers it well."

"Are you jealous, my sweetheart?" I pulled her closer, our faces shimmering in the golden shadows.

"Should I be?"

"It depends on how happy you keep me tonight."

"This is serious." She paused. "Saira and I both went to the same college, which I think you know, and I don't trust her." She paused again. "Actually my personal feelings aren't even that important. We are in a fragile spot with this hotel deal."

"Okay, so we're talking business again?"

"You're right. My apologies. We won't talk business, but all I wanted to say is, be careful with Indian media. They're vultures. They can toast a life for a story, forget about personal relationships."

"And you think Saira is going to betray us?" Ria's concerns were legit. "If I may ask, why don't you trust her?"

Ria's lack of words created a round bloated balloon of silence. "Saira is different," she finally revealed.

"How so?"

"I don't know," she confided. "Just a gut feeling. Nothing more."

"Interesting. What did you guys talk about?"

"You," Ria replied.

"What about me?"

"She wanted to make sure I wasn't thinking that you two are getting back together. And that her focus is only on doing it right by Attanooga."

"That's just odd."

"No, it isn't, especially since you didn't tell me about meeting her for lunch."

It's always bad when ladies talk. It's worse when one happens to be your ex and the other your current girlfriend. "That's trivial," I said.

"That's what she said, too," Ria paused. "Hey, listen. I know we haven't been together for long. Hell, I don't even know if we are together. So forget what I said."

"You are insulting me now," I said. "You're my beautiful angel. Always protecting me." Her face shimmered with vanity. Our feathers remained nestled in one another.

"Do you trust me?" I asked.

"I trust you. But I don't trust her," she confessed.

"Then let's cut her lose."

"Well," she said with my face gently enshrouded in her hands, her fingers caressing my hair off the face. "I'd very much like to. But I hate to admit that she can help us, too. You see, she told me about the show on your mother and, if that rolls, we can get a hell more funding for our hotel campaign." She paused. "Plus, it's a noble cause."

"Were you testing me?"

"Maybe," she said. "Now when I look into your eyes, I know, she can't come between us, not in spirit, not in thoughts, and not in words," Ria cooed. "She's just another opportunity that would be beneficial for us and, if that helps her, that's great."

"I'll talk to Veer, too," I said.

"I already did," Ria said. "He said in quotes, 'it will be a good distraction for you if you trust Saira'."

"Distraction?"

"Speaking of distraction, how about I cook you something tonight?" Ria jumped up.

"Is that your passion, cooking?"

"Not really." She puckered her lips.

"You haven't cooked? Ever? Have you?"

"I did order you breakfast the other morning!" she exclaimed.

"How about a different plan? Let's continue to leave the food to the restaurant and why don't we pick a good dress for dinner tonight?"

"Very clever. And what would your role be when I try on different dresses?"

"I'll vote."

"Vote on what?"

"The dresses. What else?" Her rosy cheeks flared up lightly. The night was about to get fun again.

Amaan

"Did I tell you that this is the neatest car I've ever sat in?" Saira seemed honest in her praise. Who wouldn't be? This winter green Jaguar E-type was a ride my grandfather got custom built in 1961. It was a big deal back in the day. It cost him five times more to get it shipped to India than the cost of the car itself. A normal person would think it was a stupid decision, but we always picked our hearts over minds.

"Thank you. Not for nothing, but this car has quite a history," I said.

She signaled her eagerness for the tale. Her excitement was vivid.

"Are you going to *tell me* the story?" Her sneer scooped me out of my own train of thoughts, which weren't very coherent, to say the least.

"So my grandfather ordered this car for the most special woman in his life."

"You do realize I grew up in the same town as you."

"What does that mean?"

"Your grandfather had many special women in his life."

"You don't think I have that trait, do you?"

"Depends on whose genes are mutating in you."

"It's my father's!"

"That ain't helping either."

"Forget the polygamist part of the deal. You're focusing on the wrong thing. Picture this; this is the car my father sat in during his wedding," I paused. "This was in a way the car my mom and dad went on their first date in." It dawned to me thereafter. I should have taken Ria out on it first.

"This is amazing. I need to take a shot of you driving in this car, on this road."

"Don't you need a real cameraman?"

"We're going digital. We'll get the lights and cameras for official interviews, but for these stock shots, I have my Canon D530." She flittered.

"Stop here!" she instructed, and I braked on the slippery single road leading up to the fort.

As instructed, I dolled up my appearance to a suave driver with aviation sunglasses, arms stretched straight onto the steering wheel as if I was to push the car all the way up to the fort.

"Where are you going there? That's dangerous!" My courage choked looking at the fenceless jute bridge to the left, but Saira walked on it like a bird.

"Don't worry, I'm a skilled mountaineer," she revealed. "I'm almost there," she yelled just as she leapt over a naked crack big enough to swallow a dog and dizzy enough to make a crow giddy. She, on the other hand, just stood there smiling on the other side, right next to the giant stone-carved statue of Shiva.

"Alright now, fire up the engine!" she said.

After several moments of photoshoot, Saira was back in the car. "That was awesome. A romantic start of a beautiful journey," she said.

"Okay, in that spirit, my lady, let me take you to our fort, the inside of it. It has a floating tale of romance stitching many generations and many of its lovers," I said.

All I needed was that husky nod and we went all the way to the grand entrance of the Teli Fort of Attanooga.

"So, tell me about your parents. When did they come to this fort, together, for the first time ever?" she said.

The anxiety built up in me like lime-scale on hard water. The floodgates were opening up. Memorialization of my mother had begun, but a conundrum also lurked alongside.

"Have you ever been to Swabhimaan Palace?" I asked.

"Yes, for the light and sound show!"

"Let me take you inside it."

"What's inside it?"

"You'll see."

Saira

"This is the most beautiful thing I've ever seen!" I was generally good at not letting my face leak emotions, but what I had in front of me was breathtaking, outrageously beautiful, and a rarity no one knew existed, not even the people of Attanooga.

The green lagoon simmered in the dim sunlight, piercing through the crystal dome.

"There are some things that we like to keep to ourselves," Amaan said.

"Can I take a video here?"

"No," he said abruptly, dashing all my hopes to capture this beauty. "Wait a little longer, and then you can." A smile sketched on my face again.

He climbed to the side and pulled the giant ropes. The ropes weren't to open curtains, because there weren't any windows. Instead, the giant chandelier on the ceiling started to sway from one side to another, spraying a silky row of petal bed on the water.

I was trying to decipher whether my eyes were open to reality or it was one of my fantasies. "How deep is it?" I asked.

"Very. An interesting fact is that the pond connects to six other ponds across the fort. This was our ancestor's design to preserve water and control flood. Think of this as a self-sustained dam."

"It's more than just that." In all the illusory, I had all but forgotten my mission of the documentary. "So you were saying the romance starts here?"

"This is the pond where the bride bathes in, before she's officially tied to our family heritage." He paused. "This was especially important for my mother as she wasn't another royal. She was…" he paused for a moment, "from the…"

"Commoner family," I finished his sentence. A weak smile appeared on his face.

The royal pathos in his light blue eyes magnetized me. "So, you're going to bring Ria here?" I asked.

"C'mon!"

"Why not?"

"We aren't living in my parents' time, where you'd have to marry the first girl you love."

"That would be me," I murmured.

"You know what I mean. I need to be certain that Ria and I are not going to have problems after the steam runs out." He paused. "It hurts, especially for the kids."

"Is that what happened between your mom and dad?" Shamelessly, I steered in my selfish direction.

He stayed quiet. I continued, "If it's any consolation, my father left us right after I was born."

He was still quiet. Perhaps trying to find the same pain in me as was in him as I told him, "My mother and I lived with my grandparents till my mother cleared her IAS exam, then we came here, left, came here again, left and are back here, for good this time; at least she is."

"It was different in our house," he spoke up.

I waived my hands toward the rolling camera. He didn't seem to mind. "My mother changed it a lot. If it weren't for her, many things would still have been the same."

"She made many things cool for this family. Marrying a non-royal became cool."

"Can I ask another question?" I said.

He nodded. "How come your mother rarely came back to visit Veer?"

"Veer came to the U.S. often. I guess she had to take care of me. Made sure I didn't disintegrate. I should go back to the med school."

"I don't know why you would want to be a doctor anyway. Why get buried in books when you're literally fed with a golden spoon."

"It's not always what it seems." I couldn't make any sense of his response. I don't think he could make any sense of it either.

"Has it got to do with your father's death?"

"I don't know." He went cold. "Let's wrap for the day." I am sure he was frantically running in the maze of his mind, but even then he offered me his hands and off we were, back down from the fort, and I, for once, couldn't wait to be back here first thing tomorrow.

Amaan

I could see the palace radiate in the darkness. It was like a breathing live creature, as were the many guards piled up on a mile-long driveway.

"Your Highness, Mr Mayor and Mrs District Collector are in the meeting lounge." The urgency of town affairs greeted me. I didn't like being involved in these affairs, and I didn't like the title of His Highness.

"Do you need me there?" I asked the turbaned guard.

"His Highness Veer has requested you to join them."

I followed him, and the hive of moments from today's trip to the fort followed me.

"You should always listen keenly to city problems," Veer had advised. "This is your kingdom and these are your people."

Today was yet another maneuver by my dear brother to fulfill my mother's last wish – do not let Amaan perish in oblivion.

"Your Highness!" Mr Mayor erected on his feet.

Mrs Gaina stood gently as well. "Hello, Your Highness."

"Mr Mayor, Mrs District Collector," I greeted.

"Please have a seat." Veer's firm gesture was strangely also comforting. It wasn't too long before the conversation resumed, but shortly interrupted by a need for Veer to step away. "My apologies, but it's time for my flight for a conference in Europe." He turned to me. "Amaan will be with you in my absence, and it will be our pleasure to be of help to our people, anytime." He paused. "Amaan, would you mind?"

"Absolutely not," I assured.

The tone of Mr Mayor had relaxed a great deal with Veer out of the room. I didn't know if it was my brother's puissant or mine lack thereof.

"It's our honour to have you with us at this time of the year, Your Highness."

"And to come to the last topic of our discussion, it would be our greatest pleasure to have His Highness Veer, and Your Highness as the chief guests for the annual *Dussehra* parade." Mr Mayor was eloquent and full of grace.

"Please call me Amaan." I didn't like the prefix. "I insist."

After initial hesitation, Mr Mayor adjusted. "Amaan, you remind us a lot of your father. He used to be involved in the smallest planning details of the Dussehra festival and always opened his heart to us." Mr Mayor was clearly the talkative one.

"How much would be okay? Based on past experiences."

"This year will be different, Your Highness, because of recent events. Perhaps a bit larger scale to compensate for the loss of spirit."

"Okay, but I still need a figure."

"Whatever pleases you, sir."

They weren't going to give me a figure. I remembered what my father once told me. "When you're a king, they expect you to make any and all decisions. Even if it's to tell them when they can be relieved for urgent personal business."

"We'll have one million sent to you by evening."

"This is too much, Amaan," Mrs Gaina interrupted.

Almost immediately, Mr Mayor sprung up. "Your Highness, thank you very much from the people of Attanooga."

I knew that I had over committed. It was an ode to my mother. Money was irrelevant.

"I'll see you tomorrow at the unveiling of your mother's statue in Cutten Bazaar then?" Mr Mayor's question had come as a bit of a surprise. I had to be with Saira for the recording.

"Is it in my schedule?" I enquired with the attentive staff, lurking on the side of the room.

"My apologies, Amaan," Mayor interrupted. "It was in your brother's schedule, and we were planning to postpone the ceremony since your brother had a conflict with his Europe trip, but he recommended that you may be able to attend in lieu of him."

"Of course!" The words dashed instantly.

I couldn't afford to show weakness in making decisions. Mr Mayor had left with a renewed strength in his legs, but Mrs Gaina stayed back.

"I'm sorry for him." She was polite.

"Nope. It's fine. It's my wish."

"I'm actually here for you and to discuss a different topic, but Mr Mayor was adamant that I accompanied him, so that explains my unspoken presence."

"Ah! And I thought it was my face!" At least that broke the ice with Mrs Gaina. She wasn't someone you could get a read on. Very layered in how she carried her inner workings.

"You know Amaan, I never looked at the mountains like this before." Mrs Gaina pointed to the flowing curtains revealing behind it the hidden peaks around the burg.

"You're embarrassing me, Mrs Gaina."

"You're too nice," she said. "Much like your mother." She paused, and then her focus turned back to the mountains. "Even the peaks have their hats shined. They're thumping their chest, for their lost heir has arrived. They'll be alps once more."

"You're very kind." I appreciated her words. "But the heir was always here."

"It's funny how we don't notice things when they're right in front of us, and one day when they disappear, they become the most important thing in our lives." She paused. "Had that ever happened to you?" I could sense that extra nervous heartbeat in her.

"What's troubling you, Mrs Gaina?"

Her words picked up pace. "I love Saira very much, like every mother. Much like your mother loved you. But sometimes too much love can become smothering. It's a fine line, but it's a line every parent walks." She paused to look away from me toward the dark clouds. "Like those clouds. They surrender to these mountains, not realizing that the mountains don't need them. They don't want to be buried in clouds, they want to rise up, shine in their tall peaks." She turned back to me. "I'm sorry, I'm talking gibberish again."

"Nope," I said instantly. "That's an intimate prognosis of a mother-child relationship."

She continued, though her mood had turned drowsy. "Saira feels like that with me. Like I'm trying to cage her. Only if she would understand why."

"Why?" I asked.

"Not all stars shine the same, and everything that shines isn't free of blemishes."

"I don't understand."

"I need you to do me a favour."

"Absolutely, anything."

"If you're able to, please stop encouraging her series on Attanooga and your father."

"I'm sorry, Mrs Gaina, you're mistaken. She isn't making a series on Attanooga or my father, per se; she's actually making it on my mother, Queen Sana."

"She told you that?"

"Yes, and it's clearly laid out as such in the contract papers." Crude remarks for her daughter shook me a bit. However, if there was a point, I wanted it noted. "I can share those papers with you, if you like."

"That will be very helpful."

"What concerns you, Mrs Gaina?"

"Nothing." She wore a forced smile. "This town, Amaan, is mystical. It doesn't let people leave, and the people who come in don't want to leave." She paused. "I'm one of those happy prisoners."

"And it looks like I'm becoming one, too." I wanted to splinter the tension, one plank at a time.

"You can't leave. That will destroy this town. While they see His Highness Veer as their leader, they see you the same way as your mother." She paused. "Your mother was the lucky charm for these people. A woman whose mission was to uplift, make them able. And now, you have the burden of every household in this town." She paused, again. "They're all looking up to you to confer the same quality into their lives again."

For the first time, a sense of responsibility was settling in. I was beginning to get the burden that my father faced, my mother acted on and my brother was living every day.

"What do you mean? The landslides? That happens all the time, though. Right?"

"You'll see tomorrow." She had turned somber, and so had I.

As I drove past the wet green sways of lanky trees, I could taste my memories from the past. Nothing had changed in this quaint town, the hamster houses, the snaky roads, the ever-misty monsoon, and the gush of fragrance of many innocent smiles. The tall mountains stood with pride, and so did the clobbered hump built from piles of rubble, one landslide at a time. It didn't sit right. A fear that a sinkhole may crack open and take it all away was more than a metaphor, at least in the fast-changing lanes of my nostalgia.

Rushed through the back entrance, I finally made it to the event. The grass in the Knight 'n' Dame Park prisoned under the feet of Attanoogians. Not even a speck dared to come to sight. Today was the unveiling of their queen's statue.

"Today, our queen stands next to our king, shoulder to shoulder, just like they partnered to uplift our town, together." Mr Mayor declared to a thunderous applause. He continued after a pause. "She raised Attanooga to the peak that we are at today." The demonstrative crowd got louder. "Without wasting much time, I'd like to invite His Highness Amaan to unveil the statue and say a few words."

His words signalled an unparalleled wave. The entire crowd stood, not withstanding even the elders. Hope flooded through their eyes, as if I was the messiah. *Was I?*

It wasn't long before I was on the podium, stared at as the messiah who would fix their lives again. My courage or lack thereof had shown its true colors. I was at a loss of words, thoughts, and sanity. My scribbled notes fled away. *I was on my own.*

Chanting of the crowd had made it impossible to speak, perhaps a good thing, considering public speaking wasn't my strongest suit. My brother best dealt it.

The will to cheer their prince and the desire to listen to my words had finally reconciled into a silence that one got only in a dreamless sleep.

It was only a few minutes into the speech that I began listening to my own words. "We will rebuild every broken brick. We will rebuild every washed away hope. Let there be no doubt that we will rebuild every young future of Attanooga that exists today and the many bright ones that are yet to come."

The crowd broke free. I wasn't on the podium, but on the shoulders of many young citizens, able to see through the thick quilt of garlands, and hope.

"Mrs Gaina conveys her regrets, for she had to leave the unveiling ceremony early," Mr Mayor whispered on our way out of the park. “She wanted to be at the landslide site beforehand to make sure things were in order for you,” he informed.

I couldn’t help look beyond him. Children had begun to peep into our car windows. Mischief and innocence both rendered flawlessly onto them. The motorcade was a celebration path. It was hard to forget, for this was a ritual best led by my father.

“How far is the site?” I asked.

“Less than a kilometer, Your Highness,” Mr Mayor responded.

“Let’s bring the roof down,” I commanded.

“Are you sure, Your Highness?”

“Yes,” I said with a smile carved in stone and a confidence built with rocks.

“Quite in contrast to the Cutten Bazaar?” Mrs Gaina quipped.

What lay ahead of me wasn’t anything particularly awful, until one looked carefully. The lifeline of Attanooga lay buried in it.

“Landslides have eradicated a large portion of industrial land,” Mrs Gaina continued.

I remembered my mother talking about it. She had pledged millions of dollars to it. “In the fear of sounding ignorant, why can’t we rebuild the industrial land?” I asked.

“We have, Amaan,” she confided. “But this is the fourth landslide in last ten years, and second in last three years.

“The new plants were re-built, and they weren’t even running for six months when the disaster struck again.” Her chi turned low again.

“Then we need to choose a different part of the town to rebuild it.”

“We’ve explored that as well.” Mrs Gaina paused. “We’re eight thousand feet above the sea level and the only commodity we can sell is our mineral water which, regretfully, can only be harvested from here.”

“How about we build a canal?”

“The next habitable land for industrial use is up higher. The cost to pump the water up would make the business impossible to conduct,” she informed.

“You’ve already considered all that, correct?” I could tell from the way she stared that these questions were already asked and answered.

“Tourism is the only thing that can save this town. The hotel deal is important,” she whispered before leaving. “Don’t let anything or anyone affect it.”

This wasn’t the sight or the responsibility I had expected. I so badly wanted to talk to Veer, but he was gone, perhaps on purpose.

“Sorry for bailing on you yesterday.” Saira and I sat atop the rampart, our heads holstered in the terreplein.

“It’s okay.” Saira pulled her head back, and so did I. “We can push it out further, if you like.”

“Can I ask you something?”

The noisy wind slaughtered my words before they could even reach Saira. “What’s wrong with the weather in this place?” she mumbled.

"Weather is one thing that's always betrayed us."

"You saw the damage from the landslides?" she remained by the side, her hands rested on mine.

"Can I trust you with this show?" I broke the patch.

"What kind of question is that?"

"I hope this sheds positive light on Attanooga."

"Of course!" I could see the confusion floating in her eyes. "Isn't that the intent?"

"Yes. It is. This town has a lot of faith in us."

"Us? Do you mean you?"

"No. I meant us. Everyone." I paused. "Your mother has made this place her religion. Never to let go of it. Always defending it."

"That I'd agree with."

"And how about you?"

"Do you have any doubt?" she asked, and so did her eyes, which stood clear of any malice.

"No," I proclaimed.

It was the truth I saw and believed in; set aside what Mrs Gaina thought.

"Don't hesitate. Ask me whatever you want. What's burning you?"

"Nothing." I was at a sudden loss of words. I feared her seeing into me. I had to move the topic away. "You're lucky to have a mother like Mrs Gaina."

"You're polite." She smirked, seeing through me again. "You haven't seen the fireworks then." I could feel her reluctance on the topic, but then she spoke candidly. "We just have each other and that creates complications."

"It's important to trust each other; otherwise, the relationship just falls apart."

"You're absolutely right. And, speaking of trust, let's move to the purpose we're here for," she said. "How did Queen Sana manage all the indiscretions of His Highness?"

"You mean the many cases of my father's affairs?"

"I didn't mean to offend by any means."

"It's fine. It was his way of life. Therefore, it's okay. Her duty was toward raising us, Veer and I, and the people of Attanooga. And that's where she focused."

"What about after your father's death? Did she try to start a new life with someone else?"

Strangely enough, this topic didn't make me cringe. She deserved a far better person than my father. I pleaded her to leave him when he was alive and, after his death, I was pleased because now she was free to find happiness elsewhere.

"I wanted her to. But she used to say, she's lived that part of her life already." I paused, reeling through many pictures of her with me.

I continued, "Maybe I made her life miserable. I'll never be able to ask her now, would I?" Saira's soft hands dug in my hair, just as she used to do when we were kids.

"I can't believe you still have this trick," I prattled to the comfort dispensed from her light massage.

"Don't tell Ria about it or she'll pluck these hairs right off your head." We both laughed. She was nothing like what her mother thought of her. I had no doubt that she wasn't scheming anything.

"Hey, do you remember when we were kids?" I asked.

"I do. But that's a bit vague reference, don't you think?"

"Well. Let me narrow it down for you. It was your birthday and you were asked for a wish." Her brows curled. "You don't remember that?"

"This is the weirdest thing. I don't remember a thing."

"I remember as a child when we used to get these monstrous wind spurts. There was something we did that'd drain our blood straight out of our skin."

"I'm not scared." Her face remained placid.

"Are you sure? This can get a little, let's just say, dangerous."

"What do you have in mind?" she asked, shifting her eyes on mine.

"Buckle up your wits. The adventure up next ain't any child's play." We were out of the car, our feet pedalling alongside a horde of birds on the other side of the tall brick boundary. I climbed up on top of the wall, and with a little pull, the warrior of Saira's soul was out in the open, her head raised to the sun in pride.

"This is how you spot a snake," I exclaimed.

"You're kidding me, right?" Her face summersaulted like a sunflower at the first sight of dusk.

"Nope, I'm not. They come out in these winds. Look at this." I picked up a stick and slowly poked through the grass until I could no longer. A fervent rustle in the bushes revealed what lay under it, a creamy three-foot long viper! Slithering faster than a horse and like a firefly, it was there, then wasn't.

"Oh my god, oh my god..." She quivered, clutching my hands, then my arms, then my shoulders. It felt like a steam of hot water in freezing cold. A feeling sketched with bright crayons.

"Alright, so what are we doing now?" she simpered after a while.

"Nothing," I whispered.

"Okay," she whispered, too. Her hands still on my shoulder, my hands on hers.

"You know the most exciting part of my life away from you?"

"Tell me."

"The worldly things didn't ink any happiness in me; it was the night, alone in my bed, ready to be with you. Dreams were all I had, but no longer today."

"What will happen today?"

"We will happen today," I hissed.

"This isn't right," she said.

"I'm not here to hurt you. This knight in shining armor costume was meant to be a metaphor coming to life!"

"I don't know if you were trying to be funny or what. But I have to tell you it was bad, really bad." She paused. "But I don't mind it. I don't mind anything about you!" She flung her arms around me, and I, like a swift magician, took her up from the feet and onto my ring of arms. A will not to unite as one had been shattered and a thirst to swim in it plunged us into the deep blue sea of forbiddance.

Saira

I didn't feel anything on my body. Not the clothes, not the shoes, not the nose ring, not the necklace. I was the happy fish who didn't mind this warm, mushy net of what had happened. I felt cared, loved. I yearned to love him more than he desired, more than I could give.

"Are you alright?" Neil's unpleasant voice had managed to scissor through.

"Yes," I sassed with a smile packed with a single message over and over again. *Leave me alone.*

"Your ecstatic face; my god, what have you been dreaming, girl?" I was wrong; he had a military grade shield against hints that signaled him to walk away along with his sleaze. At times, I wondered if it was on purpose or he actually just never got the hint.

"I was thinking about a dream I had last night."

"Was I in it?" His smile degraded into a rotten porridge.

"As a matter of fact, you were."

"Uh oh. This is getting interesting." He sunk in the chair, arms behind his head, eyes half closed. I had no idea if he was trying to teleport himself into my dream or mimicking the supernatural clown from Stephen King's novel. "So?" he murmured. "What was I doing?" he questioned, his eyes remained closed.

"I can't remember all of it, but the bits and parts that I can remember, there was a lot of bare skin around you."

"I hope it was nice smooth ones."

"It was nice. Not smooth, though. It was of a lot of hairy men in striped jail clothes." His eyes plied open. "And you know what they say of the dreams you see in the morning?"

"I do," he ranted. "And hope you got your fun."

"I swear on you," I retorted. "That's what I saw."

"And that's what you were thinking about with that orgasmic smile on your face?"

"Oh, that," I said. "No, that was a different dream in which I was with a man who had just bought me a five carat diamond."

"Whatever." He swiped open a new topic. "How are we doing with the show?"

I had that question answered much before he even asked. "It's already edited into a nice fifteen-minute slot." The one that made Neil's hair rose like a porcupine. For the first time perhaps, he didn't have much to say.

"This is really good work." His tone turned somber. "You are really cut out for this."

"Thank you," I avowed, even though I knew he said those words only because my exemplary work had thwarted his attempts to stick it with poop.

Amaan

"It'll be a few more minutes, and then we can roll." Saira's attitude was unhinged. She exhibited neither fear nor guilt. "Sorry Ria, to take your handsome prince away," she teased.

After carving a pumpkin during Christmas, Saira and I were face to face for the first time today. We had an unspoken understanding, never to talk about the incident again, as if it never happened.

That didn't mean that the maggots of guilt didn't latch onto me. Moreover, this conversation between Saira and Ria was making my skin crawl.

"No," Ria replied to Saira. "Thank you for doing this. It means a lot to us."

Only if she knew thatI had broken her faith in me, for Saira. I should tell Ria that it was a mistake, never to happen again. I had been juggling thoughts for a full hour now; hiding it under my sham smile. *This is it.* My courage knitted around the guilty rock, and suddenly it became clear; I had to tell Ria about the affair. *Right now.*

"This is the first video shoot for your mother's show. Are you ready for this?" Ria's sweet smile crushed my strength, yet again.

"Yup!" I consented.

She had no idea that a few rogue videos were already in the cans along with my irrefutable mistake. The sponge of my courage squeezed dry. I just couldn't bear to see those kind eyes in pain of my adultery. Throughout the day, Ria sat below her umbrella, patiently working on her laptop. A show of strength, support, and love. That was until she received a message on her phone. I could sense her stare even from this far off.

Something went wrong. I sped back to that night, spotting every angle of the fort.Was anyone there? A full scan came back negative. *Ease off the bullet train of guilt or there'd sure be a wreck.*

"We'll take a break now," Saira announced, her hands pressed on mine, a mellow stroke through her fingers, seemingly applauding my courage of not losing my cards while shuffling the private moments of my life.

"Sounds good," I replied, gently slipping my hand away. "I need to take a walk."

As I walked closer to Ria, her brows had retraced back in the comfort bushes. "I'll walk with you." I was stunned to hear the icy tone in Ria's voice.

I didn't let my face leak any of it. I was ready for the worst. It was show time. "Don't let Saira control you so much," she said as we strolled on the creeping bent grass in the atrium.

"Why do you say that?"

"You're doing her a favour, too, by agreeing to do this show." She wrapped her arms around mine. "This family and this town have controlled the flow of information; whether it's your mother's life or the death of your father."

"This show isn't about that. You saw the interviews, right?"

"I did." She was hesitant, and then she went dark.

She pulled her phone out and showed me a video.

"How did you get it?" I turned choleric.

"Does it matter?"

"Yes, it does." My scalp burned with rage. "Why have you been snooping around?"

"I'm not the bad one here?" she paused.

I felt like fisting the plaster out of the wall ahead. *This can't be right. There has to be another explanation.*

I was still buried deep, playing ping-pong with my own two sides of the brain, when Saira showed up. "Hello, you two! Do you mind if I join you?"

Look at her, as if nothing had happened. *How could she lie about her intentions so easily?* Her eyes were lying, her hands were lying, and I think us making love that night was a lie too.

"Well. I can smell some intense bubbles here. Everything okay?" Saira spoke again.

I had to compose myself. "You tell me," I said.

"What does that mean?" Saira's eyes rolled all the way to the left, hand in hand with her chin.

"It's nothing, Saira. Just a lover's quarrel. Can you give us a minute?" Ria intervened.

"Sure," Saira confirmed, heartbroken perhaps. *She better be.*

"We'll resume in another fifteen minutes." She walked back to her crew.

"What was that?" Ria asked a while later, with Saira well out of sight.

"What do you mean? How do you think I should react after seeing that?"

"Two things. First, we need to confirm if it's in fact what it looks like. Second and most important one, you have to bring this topic with her in private."

"What do you mean?"

"You two have a history. And she deserves to be treated fairly without the undue distraction of me or anyone else being around."

I wasn't thinking about etiquette, and I certainly didn't want to take any call now. I muffled my vibrating phone to a painless death. My sanctuary was short-lived as I saw the turbaned guard parading my way with a silver-plated cordless.

"Mrs Gaina for you, Your Highness," the staff informed me.

"I was wondering if you gave any thought to the discussion we had the other day," Mrs Gaina voiced over the phone.

"I did, and quite coincidentally I've just come across some materials that confirm your suspicions."

"I don't want to be the bearer of bad news, but," she cleared her thoughts, perhaps stacking them in the order from bad to worst. "I've just gotten to know that Saira has requested permission to visit your father's killer in prison."

That was it. I had become inept to have any coherent conversation. Not with Mrs Gaina, not with Ria. I wanted some answers, and Saira was going to give it to me right now.

"So, Saira, can we talk?" Anger fumed under my hard steps.

"Sure, we're ready to roll here, but we can spare a few."

I smiled as a bloody burned out cheetah. "Let me ask you this. What's the theme of our show?"

"That question again?" she said. "If you have to ask me something, shoot it from the hip."

I wheezed up a bucket full of air. "So you want this whole 'show' to be some sleazy fuck show of my mother with my father's murderer? Who, by the way, also happens to be a freaking menial servant in the palace."

"Hold on..." Her lost breath swallowed all the people from the room in it.

"No. YOU hold on." My teeth ruthlessly plowed one another, crashing a whole train of abuse in it. "You know what?" I had nothing good to say.

"I wonder… who are you? What are you? Do you have anything humane? Your entire charade to be nice, it's all just a façade, isn't it?" I yelled.

"You're angry right now. I'll let you speak." She stood there motionless, staring into my eyes.

I wanted to tell her how her own mother didn't trust her, how she thought of her as rotten trash, but I decided otherwise, not out of mercy for her, but because I cared for her mother. Instead, I decided to erect a wall between Saira and me, a wall of spite with the fodder of my hate.

Saira

Roped, then dragged out of my fairy tale, I was a heathen to the world and to my own selfish body. That blood in it, if tested, could only paint hate.

I wish someone put me out of this misery. *What did I do to deserve this? Was it that I longed to love, or was it that I wanted to be loved?*

"And you thought he would be different. Ha! Wishful thinking," Pison howled, her legs sharpened like a spear. "Every stab I pounce in your meat is for a misstep you took," she crackled. "Amaan is even uglier than other dogs." My skin stretched like a raw silk veil under Pison's spasms of anger.

I must stop her or else I'll implode. I slammed the door of my office, heavily stumbled down to the cabinet. My hands traced the dust in the empty shelf. *God damn it! Where is it?* The stabbing from Pison was tearing my skin apart. I had to stop her. I slid down to the last shelf, my arms stretched behind the books, and there it was, chlorpromazine, my rainy day pill.

I put it on my tongue and it found its way, slithering down, unpacking its arsenal, fuming out that blood snatcher, and returning me to calm. I could finally breathe.

My head felt so much lighter, all the pain mopping away, slowly.

"How is it going with the blue-eyed prince? What a sour waste of an opportunity." My eyes slowly opened to a loathing posture of Neil. The sun was going under the cave.

The fog was settling back in the dust. However, there was something else. Something alarming in his words. "How did you know?" I asked.

His parading stopped abruptly, which supposedly meant that his sadistic mind had turned from ecstatic to alarm. "Know what?"

The hints of his insults speared through me, crunching my bones, but today I wasn't going to let myself bleed to shame. "You know you're like one of those cute little dogs?" The pin ripped off the grenade, and before I could finish, he had to open his mouth with sub-elementary grade English.

"Well if you call me dog, I can call you bitch."

I didn't even look at his face, I was positive he was smiling. He never got mad. He was made of some fungi-laden skin that couldn't get any worse. I had to finish my insult; I couldn't let him digress. "The kind of cute dog that's stretched in the middle, and balls the size of a peanut and pissing from a borrowed dick..."

He cleared his throat. I think he wanted to say something, but he had already used half a dozen words that he knew. He still had his, "Ahm, oh," now accented with an ugly orphan tone.

"... the kind that even bitches like to fuck!" I said. There it was! I had fully vocalized by hate. The whole insult poured out of the sack and he lay buried in it. *I wish he died in it, too.*

"I don't know this person. You're out of your mind," he said. What a failed bully he was. He couldn't bully me, so now he wanted to make me feel guilty.

"You can always go to HR and tell them that a little girl called Saira fucked me up real bad. I'm scared." I felt like the blazing train that had lost its brakes. The best part was that I didn't mind at all. *All men are the same, sleazy misogynists, and the only thing that can cure them is hard-twined jute smacking by a woman.*

"I get it, you're having a bad day, and I'll leave you alone." He slyly walked away, with the hangover of the last few minutes.

Amaan

I raced past the Japanese garden, around the Koi, and into the grand foyer on Astoria house in the palace.

"His Highness is a bit upset," the guard outside, whispered.

Nothing in this part of the palace smiled today. Hordes of staff were running like a bunch of headless chickens. Even the flowers ducked away at the sight of anything human.

It was my turn now.

"How can she do this?" I had no good answer to the first question from Veer. Ria and I barely looked at each other. She was so submerged on the phone, I could run a ship over her, and she wouldn't even blink.

"People change," I replied to Veer. "It's been ten years, and we have no idea what her priorities are."

"But her mother, Mrs Gaina is so loyal to Attanooga." He had to sip a few more mojitos to shelf the reality in his head.

"She is," I replied.

"We have to loop her in. She might know what the hell Saira is up to."

Ria's cryptic conversation in a remote corner of the room ended, and the way she was walking toward us, an invisible balloon of grave disappointment followed her every step. *What else could we have unearthed about Saira?*

"I have some news," Ria announced.

Veer flapped his hands in dismay. "What else did we find?"

"It's not exactly about Saira, but it's related. Taj wants to extend the deliberation period a bit longer."

"So, what's the big deal?" Veer asked.

"They want it extended by two years." Ria's politeness should have helped with the message, but it didn't.

"That's ludicrous! Why?"

Ria let the silence speak.

"Because of this stupid TV show? That's even more preposterous. How the hell do they know about the video?"

"The trailer was leaked on YouTube," Ria mumbled.

"How?" Veer was full of rhetoric, rightly so, just as I was foaming in froth of my own sins. *I let her in our lives. What a fool I was.* "How many people have watched?" he asked.

"Not too many," Ria clarified. "I just spoke to our technology team and they've already filed a request to block it."

Veer spoke up, "This freaking digital age, everything leaks out in no time." He paused. "Let me ask this. Who cares about a stupid TV documentary? Hell, how many people in today's generation even know what a documentary means?"

"Your Highness," Ria spoke softly. "We've run digital campaigns for 'Shinier with you' and that spread quickly. People accessing digital channels know of this town and, going by the chatter on internet, there's a lot of sticky interest."

"What does that mean?" Veer asked.

"That means that a lot of people are subscribed to keywords such as #Attanooga. And we should assume that all of them have access to the video."

"Doesn't mean they saw it." Veer's cut throat politician acumen had gone for a toss.

"The comments have already begun to fill on the video. And they aren't good." Ria dropped her tone straight to the floor.

"What do they say?"

"It's best to not discuss it. They could be paid trolls by your opposition."

"I want to know," Veer demanded.

"Creepy queen must be high on that potion!" Ria read out a comment and stayed quiet. Veer's persistent eye's signal was clear. Go on. "Another one. This is the last place I'll go. I'd rather go to Bangarh fort and get tortured by its ghosts," she mumbled.

"Enough!" I avowed. "What's the status? Is the video blocked yet?"

"Let me check!" Ria pulled the screens. "Still in process."

"Amaan, can you please take care of Taj?" Veer said.

I wasn't thinking about the hotel deal or Taj. This was my mother whom the public was humiliating.

"I'll try to get them back on the table," Ria came to my rescue.

"Thanks, Ria." Veer was gratuitous. "And I need to know how this got out. I want no more leaks."

"Got it, Your Highness." Ria turned to me, waiting for my consent, too. But my mind was busy trying to make sense of all this mess.

"So tell me, what exactly happened here?" Veer's eyes darted on Ria.

"What do you mean?" she bemoaned.

"What led to this leak? Who leaked it?"

"I have my suspicions," she blabbered.

"It's Saira," I announced.

Ria's body language flooded with objection, but her words remained absent, atleast for a few seconds. "I think so, too." Ria later acknowledged, adding a bucket full of hot blood in Veer's nerves.

"People, we have our state elections in less than five months. This could change everything. We're saying that every town of the state will be like Attanooga. If we can't fix it, the whole story crashes and burns, and so will our aspiration to rule the entire state."

We hadn't even spun to the bottom of the hour and the consortium of Veer's inner circle was gathered in the Astoria house, undecided on how to put out a wildfire with a cup of water.

"I warned Amaan about what was going on, and I thought we put a lid on that," Mrs Gaina announced.

"We did," I chipped in. "I don't think the problem will expand anymore."

"We need a plan B," Veer announced.

"Plan B for Saira?" I said.

My question put me squarely in the firing line from Mrs Gaina.

"If this hotel deal blows up, I need a parallel narrative on how this state will live up to the 'Shinier with you' goal." Veer conceded even before Mrs Gaina could speak up.

"Amaan, I need you to come up with alternate plans to counter, now that the whole world knows about it."

"Mrs Gaina, why is Saira doing all this?" Before Mrs Gaina could answer, Veer blurted again. "Actually, I'd just like to contain it, whatever it takes."

"Yes." She was hesitant.

"Everything okay?" I asked her softly.

"Nothing. I have this covered." She seemed filled with a strange remorse.

"Let me talk to the channel. We need to get that goddamn video off the internet." Veer had moved on.

"Ria and Amaan, I need you to set up a meeting with Taj and let's have our Plan B ready by then. Hope that will reassure them. I want the Taj flag here in a month. Let's get to work, guys." Veer clapped the meeting to closure.

Saira

That's how it was ten years ago, when I first stepped into the shit-coloured concrete basement in my mother's house. The lone bulb flickered to remind that the stairway to hell had no railings and the bottomless dark pit was ready to swallow flesh. Also, the perfect storm for the despicable Pison to spin out.

Her serpentine spine-crawling sensation, resurrecting my demons, telling them, "Be careful! Watching they are, staring they are, don't turn!" She dug her stinger, forcing me to turn, forcing me to burn until there was nothing left; no flesh and no bones.

I had to weaponize, pick something, anything that would save me from the monster. My hands shuffled through the dust, grabbing nothing. *Is today the day, when I die?*

"Not today," I said to myself, "Not today." I dug my hands deep and wide until my fingers crashed on the stained iron bar. Now, I was ready. *No one can run over me anymore.* Here comes the creak on the door, here comes the shadow. All right, showtime. Three... two... one... boom! *Die, you monster!*

"Mommy! What are you doing here?"

"Oh, god." My mother was still wheezing in her bid to defuse all the air she had swallowed. "What the hell did you intend to do with that weapon?"

"Can't you knock?" I blustered.

"Knock for what? This is my home." The yellow peel of her face had finally begun to drown in a fresh flow of calm blood. "So, even when you accept my invitation, you choose not to let me know in advance when you'll arrive."

"I decided to give our relationship another chance." The lipstick on words smudged under my unrelenting hate for my mother. "That alone should be enough."

I was the rooster melting in rage for failing to wake an owl.

She responded with a familiar pale smile.

"I'm kidding." I felt the urge to reverse my attitude. "And thanks for the invitation."

She scarfed through my words, seemingly weighing every drop of my ill intentions. "Come up when you're done. I'll get some food prepared, if you're planning to stay for dinner."

She trudged up the basement stairway when I apprised her. "I'm not going to stay here more than a few days."

Her steps stopped. "This is your home. I'm just glad you're here." She didn't even look back when she blabbered. There must be something short in my wiring. *Why can't I keep up relationships?* I couldn't keep Amaan back then, hell not even when I got another chance. Colleagues, friends, family, my own mother. Couldn't even do that well. *I must be the cursed black widow.*

To add fuel to the fire, if one thing my mother knew, it was how to make me drench in guilt. Everything in the house was perfect. Designed for my happiness. My bedroom didn't have even a grain of dust; the walls smelled of roses, the bed wore fifty-six threads of fresh linen. I had to admit I was at the cusp of happiness; ready to forget my past few days.

"I'm sorry, Mommy, for earlier," I said.

"It's okay," she said, as the waiter brought in piping hot *aloo methi, paneer, nan and lemon rice*.

I sat doused in guilt again. Moments of our past jumped into my eyes. Like the last time she had come to Delhi, I had decided not to meet her. Why? Because I didn't want to. That's it. That was my reason.

Enough of the past. I couldn't live in it when I had her right in front of me. "I want us to be close, Mommy."

She rubbed her hands on mine, tapping it with a lullaby tune.

"I still remember you and I in the park, running, dancing. How old was I?"

She sketched a smile. "You were six then." She looked up, nuzzled my hair, then her hands got jammed in the past. "I had just gotten the letter that I had made it to IAS."

"You were so excited." I paused just to relish that smile on her face. "You danced till Grandpa pulled the plug off that stereo."

"I was silly," she admitted.

"You were fun!"

"I was just twenty-four then."

"I'm twenty-four now, and look at me! I am not half as fun as you were, and I don't have a yapping six-year-old to deal with."

"Maybe that's what you need. A six-year-old."

"Stop it, Mommy!" A simmering feeling of real happiness blushed my cheeks. "Thank you for bearing with me."

"Are you insane?" My hand in hers was just so comforting. "You're just like me at that age. A body full of cynicism and a mind full of hope."

What she said felt right, but I could never be like her. She was so much better than I was. *Was it this jealousy that painted the rift between us*?

Now was a real chance to put the plaster on our fractured relationship. As they say, someone's sorrow is another's laugh. In this case, I was the former and the latter.

"Aren't you going to ask why I agreed to come here?" I asked later when I was in the bed.

"I know you will tell me when you think you have to." She turned off the lights. "Good night, my baby."

She wasn't too happy in the morning. I could smell it. She hadn't come to wake me up. She didn't mind me coming in my pajamas to the living room, too. "Everything okay, mommy?" I asked.

"Yeah, baby. Everything is fine." She was still all smiles. Between bites of her hasty breakfast, she pulled the ring and ordered a cup of tea for me.

"Can I ask you something?"

"Sure," she replied.

"How loyal do you think this town is to the royal family?"

She looked up. "Why do you ask?"

"I'm sure you know about the documentary and the news."

She remained placid, her face devoid of any wrinkles.

"So, what do you think?" I asked again. "And just so you know, I had nothing to do with that YouTube leak."

"I trust you," she said.

That was strange. This must have been the quickest agreement we had gotten since forever.

"But that doesn't mean that the fingers aren't pointed at you," she conceded.

"These people have been here forever. Their DNA has seen wars, war crimes, slaughters, slavery, and one person who always stood by them is their king, their protector. They wouldn't see it any other way. Even if the truth, which I believe, is something else."

"What's the point?"

"The point is you can break a mind, a heart; you can't break a tradition that's so deeply rooted that it shapes the eyes and the ears of this community."

"Right! And that's why I will."

"You'll what?" Her eyes flew right into mine.

"I'd like to get their opinion."

"Don't do that." Her voice turned stiff. "The fury you'd face will burn everything in it."

"I want this to be real, the one that connects with people. There's nothing wrong in getting their anger on tape."

"It's not them I'm worried about," she bemoaned.

"It's strange that even though the queen wasn't here much, at least, not in public." I paused. "How come everyone worships her?"

The thought had banished all words from our thoughts, hers and mine.

"Can you do me a favour?" she asked.

"Sure," I assured.

"Can you drop this show?"

A hidden little animal in my mind was beginning to jump onto the seesaw of worth-it or not-worth-it.

"I can't just drop the opportunity. This is my first own show." I finally broke the seal.

"Of course not,"she replied curtly. "Then just don't bring it up here with the people of Attanooga."

"Does that include you?" I asked.

"No," she replied after a long pause.

"You were here, right? When Queen Sana left this town."

"What's your question?"

Her hesitance wasn't shying away, but so wasn't my persistence. "Did you know her? What was her state when she left?" I asked again.

"She was devastated, like anyone would be who had just lost her husband."

"Why did she leave, though?"

"She had lost her husband to death from a brutal attack." Her words slowed down.

"You're right, I suppose," I said.

"Why don't we go on a vacation?" My mother decided to cut the conversation onto a different bypass. "I've been pushing an honoree invitation from a beach town in Kerala. Maybe we can go there after I come back from Delhi."

"No way!" I smiled. "I have so much work."

She had seen through me. "I have a commitment, Mommy. I'm a journalist. I can hibernate. But I can't give up."

"Then make use of your hibernation." She smiled. "Maybe we'll find someone suitable for you there."

"Stop it!" Can't stop a mother from worrying.

There was also something else that couldn't be stopped; not by her, not by me, not by anyone else.

Amaan

"I'm sorry, Amaan," Ria drawled. "I know how unnecessary this whole situation is."

"It's my fault." I had to channel it back. Just to lighten my chest.

"It's not your fault." Her warm fingers skirted over mine. I felt protected. More so, as the chopper wasn't mid-air anymore. We were firmly on the terrace of the ITC Maurya in Greater Kailash, Delhi.

"Let's not forget that unfortunately, our boring romance feeds off these boring meetings." She giggled, delighting my mood, if only for a moment.

"Thanks for lending your chopper, by the way." I smirked.

"You should be nice to your brother. Maybe he'll let you use his next time." She chuckled back.

Now was the time for some numbers to crunch and some egos to fluster. The line in the sand was getting thinner and thinner. The session thus far was fighting over the last coca cola, but what we needed was the entire rainforest.

"Here's the roadmap and profitability of the hotel," said the Taj lawyer. "If you can look at the page two, executive summary." He snooped his eyes as if the next turd out of his mouth would be an instant reaction and not a well-prepared statement, as was the case. "Our business case for this hotel is promising, but not exhilarating."

In this room full of Brooks Brothers suits, I was like a fly on the wall. Ria, on the other hand was full of electricity, the kind that thundered when touched. "So how many of these hard benefit levers have we accounted for?" she entreated.

"If you go to Appendix A, you see that we've accounted for the upcoming plan for the airport, the expansion of national highways, and the tourist growth because of affiliation with Bollywood." The Taj lawyer drew up the plan.

"So what's the trouble then?" Ria quipped.

"All the levers we have are tied to additional infrastructure development, anticipating that His Highness Veer will, you know, be the leader of the state and approve the funds."

"And he will," I chipped in.

"Absolutely, Your Highness. But this story can dent a lot."

"We have control over it. We've already blocked it on YouTube. Correct, Ria?"

"Absolutely!" Ria's confident nod was much needed.

"I'm sorry, Your Highness. We're no experts at this. But our social media team tells us that the videos have been uploaded at a dozen other sites and has already crossed millions of views on Instagram and Facebook." My jaws crushed inside my mouth, my brain sparked a misfire of anger. This new development was news to me.

"We're over-thinking this one," I said.

The Taj lawyer instantly picked up the ridiculousness of my brash comment. "Your Highness, there's nothing except for the heritage, which alone can or could attract tourists."

His bitter statement was also true.

The chatter in the room had fizzled. Silence isn't always bad. At times, it could be enduring, like a pond of still water. Every stone you throw designs a unique reflection.

"If you'd like us to jumpstart, we can still do it." The first positive comment of the day from them reignited Ria.

"Let's talk about it," Ria intervened.

"We need to revisit the terms of the deal."

"Which ones to be specific?" Ria asked.

"Right now, the lease we have is fixed at one million per year for the first ten years. We can pay all of it in advance and buy the palace outright."

"Ten million dollars? You must be kidding." I was furious.

"We're just exploring options here." Ria rescued the dialogue on my behalf. "We have to be reasonable about it. We're talking about a one thousand acre plot of historic significance, then..."

"Stop it!" I fussed. "We're not selling the palace. Period."

"We understand that it's a big decision." The lawyers stood. "Why don't we think about this and perhaps come up with some other options, too, if feasible."

"You can vet some options from your side and we can see what else we can look into." Ria concurred.

It wasn't very long after they were gone that Ria and I were at odds. "How could you even entertain that idea?" I asked.

"We have to keep all options on the table." Her attempts to pacify me were falling off the tree like red leaves in the fall. "It doesn't mean we have to agree to it."

"These guys are trying to squeeze us," I goaded. "They don't care about anything. While my family is getting buried in a marsh, for them it's a freaking business opportunity." I let my words spit anger instead of the tone. "Why do we need them anyway?"

"Because they're the most prestigious group in India."

"Let's talk to Marriott, Hilton, too."

"We did," she expanded. "They all mandate that the property be developed and renovated by the owner."

"What's the cost for that then?"

"The cost for this one is around two hundred thousand dollars per room with a total of eighty million for 400 rooms." She paused. "And it's not just Attanooga. Taj is committing to buy and develop properties in five other cities."

"And, now my dear friend Saira has screwed this over," I spoke up.

"She has no idea of the damage she can cause. If not controlled, this will screw over the growth plan for an entire state. For what?"

"A stupid gossip story." My hate for Saira just shot through the stratosphere. An irrational, senseless, immature imbecile that she was!

"I'll be the last person to suggest this," Ria paused to get a gauge on my reaction thus far.

After perhaps tipping on the right side of the scale, she continued. "It may make sense for you to talk to her again."

"You gotta be kidding me!" All my seething bombs exploded.

"Have you spoken to her since that day?"

"No. And, I don't intend to."

"There's a good chance she could be convinced, if she knew what's at stake here. Maybe she just doesn't know at all."

"Didn't Veer ask Mrs Gaina to handle her?"

"She clearly doesn't listen to her mother and doesn't give a damn about anything else. I do think she listens to you."

"How can she help anyway?" I asked. "The video is out there! Right?"

"It is. But I'm sure she can do something. She can certainly refute the legitimacy of it. She can come up with a new version of it, blaming the old one on an overzealous staff member," she continued softly. "I hate to say this, but this may turn out to be good for us."

I didn't like her comment. At all.

"Then, why can't we just go to her bosses and have them fix it?" I didn't want to talk to Saira again.

"We've tried," Ria said.

"What happened?"

"Veer is trying to persuade." She stopped. "It's not looking too promising."

"Well then, we'll pay for the renovation ourselves," I announced.

"I'm not too worried about renovations," she implored. "My father can take care of that."

"I think we can manage these ourselves," I shot back.

"Your family has a lot of responsibilities. Business is just going to add to that. My father does this for a living. He builds up businesses, invests in private equity."

"That's very kind of you, Ria." I paused. "We'll see. Perhaps later."

"Amaan, listen to me," she politely interjected. "The reputation of your family is what makes or breaks Attanooga and the entire state with it. Our real option is Taj. We need the brand. We have to keep the deal alive. So it's either losing the palace, or the elections, or trying for Saira to change her mind."

Her words sunk in much slower than her pace. There was a lot in it that I didn't understand, and many new questions had splashed the floor. It was time to have a conversation with my brother.

Saira

"Ma'am?" The security guard's tone was strict. "Slip please?"

"Oh yes. Here you go!" *Buckle up girl; show them how fearless you are.*

"This letter doesn't have a date. We can't accept it," the security guard barked.

"I think my mother just forgot to put a date on it."

"Your mother?"

"Yes, I'm Mrs Gaina's daughter."

"Sorry, ma'am. I still can't let you in."

"C'mon, is there anything you can do? She'd be upset if she finds out that you didn't let her daughter in."

His salt and pepper moustache didn't move a rabbit's foot when he spoke. "We can try to call your mother."

"Sure. Why don't you do that?" I kept up my act of a brat.

The guard began dialling the number. "Sorry, ma'am. It's going to voicemail."

"It's a cell number," I blurted. "Why don't you SMS her?"

The guard looked at me as if that would give him some inspiration to make a decision. Finally, his lollygagging ended with a text through his toadstool nails.

Several moments of empty naught had passed. Nothing had come yet. Tense air had circles around us, until the phone buzzed. "Go ahead. Yes!"

"Okay, ma'am. We'll have a constable accompany you." The guard eased, signalling a constable to come forward. Within minutes, the constable and I were on our way to meet Durga when a familiar voice called us from the back.

"Ma'am!" I froze under the ice of my sweat. *Shit, did he find out?* Every step he took rung louder and louder, then there were none. He was breathing right next to me.

"You forgot your phone, ma'am." He smiled and handed over my phone, and possibly my life.

I glided past the walls stung with essays of hate, every corner captured with vicious animals, waiting to grab me; they had already snatched me in their evil eyes.

❖

"Hello, Durga." One look at the supposedly most vicious prisoner, and all the apprehensions melted.

He stood an arm away and a hand shorter, his back meandered in age.

He must be a patsy for the criminal I came to meet. *Is this a trap?* I thought.

He sat opposite me with his arms chained to the metal table. His mangled face wandered in me. His eyes blinked profusely, as if they were trying to extract me from somewhere in his past.

I plowed through his parched skin. He and I were no different. The indistinct recognition that I had seen him before splintered off a bundle of broken shards. I still hadn't put it all together.

"School," he said.

"I always thought he was a mute." The constable provided his unsolicited colour, but I punched it back to him with an ugly stare. "What, ma'am? This guy hasn't spoken a word in a decade."

"Right!" I steered back at Durga. "Now I remember. You drove me and Amaan to school!" I remembered him now, and quite strangely, that memory hauled a curvy smile along.

His dry body shuddered a bit.

"You were our guardian," I said. My hands fell onto his, and in that instant, his tears begun to snake down to the floor. The floodgates were about to be breached.

"Saira ma'am." He had finally mouthed my name in his smile. His legs charged to move to me.

"Keep your distance," the constable thundered at him.

Durga clutched my hands in fear. I didn't flinch.

"Do you want to know why I'm here?"

He nodded. Joy dripped under my hair, and a canister full of pneuma detonated.

"I'm making a show on Queen Sana."

"Show?" he mumbled.

"Think of it like a movie, but it will only come on TV."

"Telefilm?" he questioned softly.

"Yes, there you go. It's a telefilm," I rejoiced. "And, I wanted to interview everyone who knew her." The hesitance crawled back onto his face. "I've interviewed Amaan, too. Would you like to see some footage of that?"

It was only after he had seen the footage that his jim-jams surrendered. For the first time today, a real smile carved his face. "Amaan baba was always so kind. Always cared like a true king." His words bubbled with water. "Even taught me how to sing in English."

"He is." I hid my scorn deep in my skin. "So, let me ask you this first. Do you remember dropping us to school?"

He nodded. "Yes, ma'am."

"If I remember correctly, you used to take us in that black Mercedes?"

"That was the car, ma'am."

"But I also remember a white Audi."

"That was His Highness's car," he blurted.

"The royal family had so many cars. I was always confused."

"Black car was Queen's; white car was His Highness's."

"You mean it was Queen Sana's car?"

His head jogged in agreement.

"Were you her driver?"

His shut eyes bowed again. "I was Amaan baba's driver for the Queen."

"Now let me ask you about Queen Sana. Is that okay?"

"Yes," he assured.

"What was she like?" I asked.

"You," he replied.

"Sorry?"

"She was like you," he replied.

Before I could carry on with my questioning, my cell phone buzzed again. *Suri.*

"Saira, where are you?" he blurted.

"Hello to you, too, Suri." I was pissed at his lack of bedside manners. "I'm just home at Attanooga." I paused. "Working on the story."

"Hmm... Listen, get away from where you are right now." He was twitchy.

"Why?"

"I can't say it on the phone. But walk away." His words once again soused in anxious gravy.

"Sure," I replied before I heard the loud disconnect tone. He didn't even know how to say goodbye.

"Ma'am!" The constable next to me alerted me. "We have to go, ma'am. Supervisor has asked me to take you directly to him."

I heard the hasty order from the constable, but it wasn't in the front and center of my mind just yet. It was Durga's narrow humming.

"Eight angels and a pig
Let them come and take your toys
But find a safe and hide your joys
Don't you weep... don't you sleep
If eyes shut and thoughts don't fit
Wake up and dig... Wake up and dig
Remember the doll, don't forget the wig..."

Durga's humming smoked me gray. With every recitation, the smoke grew thicker, wider, dissolving my bones, my flesh, and my eyes.

"Stop this nursery rhyme!" Constable's voice rang with authority, and my eyes plied open. "And you, ma'am, time over. Let's go!"

I suspected that the shitstorm had begun. We marched off the corridors, but this time I didn't notice anything but the main gate that was getting closer and closer.

As soon as I reached the gate, the constable looked into the cabin. "The boss isn't here. Wait here, ma'am. I'll be right back," he commanded.

"Okay. Can I be back from the restroom?" I asked, which he hesitantly agreed, but then ended up showing me the way toward it.

As soon as he was out of sight, I sprinted for the first opening and I was out of that place, pacing furiously to my car.

I quickly slid into my car. I had to run from this strange land. Nothing in it felt safe, nothing in me felt safe. The feeling that someone was following me had returned. All I felt was a dark shadow of a slimy monster that strangely looked like me, spoke the same words as me, even had my nose. *It was out to get me*.

I had been dried out of air, my back hanging out of seat, my eyes frozen just below the rear-view mirror, and arms stiffened like pillars of a collapsed bridge. I slammed the gas, pulled my car out to throttle. I rammed through, onto the street, and then crushed the gas as hard as I could.

Amaan

I couldn't remember when I lay my hands on a cabinet full of documents. There had to be a unicorn idea to refurbish Attanoogians. All I had to do was to frog my way to it. One file at a time.

"Where's the short version of all this?" I questioned myself while burning the midnight oil. *Think like this is the unfound land by Columbus. If he had come here, what would he find that could make a great story to magnetize other good people to want to come to this place?*

The incessant phone flashed Saira's name, again. Sixth time in the last ten minutes. I was done with her, through and out. As Veer had said, there are more solutions than meet the eyes. I was resolute that Saira wasn't it. I slammed the button, only hoping I could appease my vengeance with a grand old slam of a steel rotary phone, but a push button would do too. *Rest in peace, Saira.*

So where was I? Columbus, right. I turned a box full of Attanooga pictures on the table, carousing through every captured angle of Attanooga. *How about we convert the downtown into a thematic shopping destination?* It didn't take too long to figure out that it was already baked in the Taj estimates.

How am I supposed to invent the unicorn?

The night at 2 a.m. was still young. I wasn't going to give up easily. It was time to look at Attanooga from every corner in these pictures. Much later, from the veil of seaweed crust appeared a flash of the white unicorn. A tingle buzzed my toes when I finally saw it. *How could no one think of it?*

Saira

Someone's walking steps on the roof woke me up. The power was out, too.

I rushed down the stairs to the basement in the house, my arms gashed by the grouts on the cemented steps, my head transmogrified into a pit of golf ball size bumps.

You're just being paranoid. I hoped the phone rang and the power company apologized for the blackout. Just then, a sharp metal rustling sound re-echoed. This was more than copper pipes expanding on hot water. *What if someone was trying to open the hatch?*

You are a fighter, and fighters strike back! A water drip sound and my heart once again dangled out of the cage and hung like a crab on a fishing pole. With vapor strength, I turned back in hush steps toward the sink. My shivering arms reached to the faucet, finally managing to turn it shut. No more blood leaking taps.

I still had to get to the hatch. *C'mon, you can do it! You're a brave girl. Remember how you trap those monsters on the show? This is no different.*

I rammed through the dark passage stumbling on the wall full of sticky note boards, my skin roughed against the wall flooding the blood red gashes with stabbing pain.

I snatched some scant air back in my chest, but not for long. It was the horrific buzzing on my phone.

"Hi, Mommy!" I cleared my throat to hoot all the anxious monsters out of me.

"Are you okay, Saira?"

"Yeah." I had to go on mute to take a deep breath. "Why do you ask?"

"It was your voice on the phone."

"Oh nothing. I just woke up."

"Right now? It's one a.m."

"I didn't realize that. Must have been all the television I watched last night."

"Saira." Her long drag of silence never came alone. "We need to talk."

"What's going on?"

"You know what's going on." She groaned.

"I'm at a loss here."

"You knew I'll be in Delhi, and what you've done today is not only unethical, but also unworthy of a daughter."

I stayed quiet.

"You forged by signature and hacked my phone. Did you really think that I won't get to know?"

"Quite the opposite actually. I knew you'd know. Just like you got to know the first time I applied to visit Durga."

"What have you become, Saira? I'm your mother."

"For once you could have tried to help your own daughter, but instead you chose to suck up to your so-called His Highness."

"Shut up!" she yelled, perhaps for the first time in as long as I could remember.

"Truth always comes in a bitter wrap."

"You have no idea what being a mother is like, do you?"

"Really? You're going to play the mother card now."

"What's wrong with you?" she hollered. "We were finally making some progress. Why do you hate me so much?"

"Let's see now. First, because of whatever the hell you wanted to do, you would dope me with sleeping pills, and now I'm addicted to it. Second, you'd beat the shit out of me so much that I'm also on painkillers. Third, you'd chase every boy away who was even an inch close to me."

"What's gotten into you? Do you have any idea what you're saying? It makes no sense."

"Really?"

She cut me off. "Are you off your vitamins?"

"There you go! Vitamins; what a show you put up; filling me up with sleeping pills, then shoving vitamins to make it better. Why didn't you just kill me if you hated me that much?"

I could hear her corrode behind the hung ringtone. Moments later, the tap walking sound rustled louder and louder and louder.

Amaan

The wind under the blades signaled an un-rung bell that the royalty was on the move and weaved in a beady necklace of one phone call to another, loading up of lithium cylinders, cranking up the voyeur lenses, and smoky peddling of the media caravan.

"I am sorry for you, Mrs Gaina." Veer thrummed at the front porch of the hospital.

"Thank you," she said softly as she shielded her face from the burning lenses. She had lost the shimmer that often graced her face. I was trying to figure what exactly she was thinking, but I couldn't.

"We promise that whosoever has committed this heinous act will be brought to justice," Veer shouted, trying to get his phony message across.

Mrs Gaina smiled gratitude. "Thank you, Your Highness!"

I had to intervene. "Brother, I think we should go inside."

"Of course," he consented, but then turned to the media herd. "Saira is in coma, but alive. Please allow the family to be alone in this hard time. I thank you all."

The waiting room felt much warmer and quieter. "If it's okay with you, I have to excuse myself from a few responsibilities until Saira is better." Her voice had tired.

"Of course, Mrs Gaina. You need not ask my permission." Veer paused. "I wish this time on no one, and please let Amaan or me know anything we can do to help."

"If it wasn't for Amaan, she could have been in a lot worse spot," she said.

"We always were here for you, Mrs Gaina. I wouldn't commoditize your loyalty by mentioning it here. But please know that you're family to us, and we'd do anything for you, much like you've done for us in the past, and I'm confident would continue to live on once Saira is better."

Mrs Gaina stood like a lioness. Listening keenly, acknowledging, but was she? I looked her in the eye, and we both shook our lashes. Seemingly, we both had our demons to hide.

"Forget about everything, Mrs Gaina. Until Saira recovers, you're invisible to us. Whatever you say or do, we wouldn't accept. In fact, we'd consider that as an insult," I declared, well judging that Veer had his mouth full of words ready to faucet.

"Absolutely." Veer surprisingly agreed, painting his full lips red.

"Let's get to hunt the perpetrator," Veer declared.

"She has been a fighter," Mrs Gaina's words came out greased in pride. "Not all of those bruises are from a fall, according to the doctor," she continued.

"How are her bones?" Veer quipped.

"She fell from the second floor and onto the bushes," Mrs Gaina said after a long pause. "Doctor is saying that's what saved her. My poor baby! What can I do to keep her away from trouble?"

"Don't worry, Mrs Gaina. We'll be personally looking after Saira. Past is past, but an event like this, we can't break away," Veer reaffirmed his stake. "Amaan, you and Ria know Saira best." I wasn't sure where he was going with this. "From today onward, Amaan and Ria will personally be by her side every day, even if it's for an hour a day," Veer declared, well noting that the media outside the window had their ears and noses buried in the conversation.

"Absolutely, brother," I replied. My arms were twisted to face Saira on a daily basis. It wasn't going to be easy. My demons clawed up to my ears. Now I had to fight them.

Amaan

"It's been less than a month, and Saira's case is already the most talked about on the internet." Ria's elated words echoed to the high point ceiling in the palace dining room.

"How so?" I asked.

"We've been publishing daily updates. It's like a real-life soap opera! And you're one of the favourite heroes!"

"Me?"

"The caring prince, who moved mountains to move Saira to the best care facility in the country!" She smiled ear to ear.

"Anyone would have done the same."

"We aren't revealing too many details on the net, though, correct? It could hurt the investigation," I said.

"It's redacted. But they know that she can move her finger now," she rambled. "Progress cultivates trust, and trust of the public is coming back. That's what we need the most."

"True, and I'd be the last soul to say this, but we do care about the victim, too, even if she isn't our best friend."

"Of course." Ria's eyes squinted, a sign that she felt offended. *I shouldn't have been so sarcastic.* "You did your part and I've been visiting her every day I'm in Delhi. It's just so hard to look at her lying there like a squash." She tunneled into a dark zone. It was almost poetic to see her mourn for her archrival. It was yet another glinting trait reaffirming her kindness to humanity.

"Good evening, Ria. Good evening, brother." Veer made his entry felt in the room when he took his designated seat at the head of the hundred-seat palace dining table. It was a sumptuous setting for dinner, a commonality in our father's days. I despised it then. Now, I was just indifferent. The rebellious thoughts didn't matter anymore. The problems today were more real.

"The favourable news has turned the polls." Ria quickly jogged back to the stuff that mattered.

"And what about the Taj deal?" he asked.

"They're still a bit in the safety bunker, so to speak."

"Why?"

"They see the polls, but it hasn't convinced them," she said.

"They're not politicians," I intervened.

"What do you mean?" asked Veer. "We've done everything to find the perpetrator for the very person who the world thinks was out to get our family." He paused. "That's common sense. Not politics."

"Yes," I acknowledged. "But they might also think that we created this whole situation in the first place."

"There will always be fiction fans," Veer said.

"On a different note, I don't even think that's the real issue we face."

"What do you mean?" Ria and Veer spoke at the same time.

"In the aftermath of this unfortunate video leak, one thing Taj did well is to make us question. What are we really doing with Attanooga?"

"We're helping our people," Veer said.

"Yes." I paused. "And with a noble thought. But not with enough thought in how to do it."

"What do you suggest?" Veer asked.

"To the purpose of this meeting then. A month late, but still fresh," I announced, and it was time to unravel the plan, to be the Columbus that would make Attanooga shine and intoxicate tourists to beeline for something a lot more than heritage sightseeing.

"Let's roll," Veer announced. "What have you got?"

Acute attention hijacked the next few minutes. Much above the threshold, I imagined. I hoped I lived up to my brother's expectations, as he did for me, when he got me out of the no-fly-list mess.

Deafening silence in the room was a first. The occasional stabbing of steel had also come to a standstill. No one was eating, no one was breathing; they were just listening to the pitch.

"This is absolutely fabulous," Veer exclaimed at the end. "We got to work the details, but I like the soul of the idea. It's a breakthrough!"

I didn't speak, but acknowledged. I had found my shine, as my mother would have said it. *I had become worthy of the family, as a leader.*

"Our Gorkha Twin Peaks will be the Ski Cliff!" Veer raised the toast. "To Attanooga, the first ski range of India, and who knew you only need a bit of snow, rest we can make our own!" He quickly snapped the drink in. "And let's have those Taj guys chip in for all the equipment too. Otherwise they can bid goodbye!"

Ria's hands squeezed in mine, and her pride in me felt misty through her kiss. I also missed someone else today, perhaps the person who, if I recall now, was the first ever to suggest this idea – Saira.

Amaan

"Hello, sir. It isn't visiting hours yet." The nurse's authority at AIIMS hospital crumbled the moment she saw a barrage of photographers chasing me.

"These vultures. Let me see what I can do," she said.

Moments later, she was back. "Just give us a few minutes. We have to change the sheets."

"Take all your time," Ria slurred to the nurse, pulling me away from the corridor and from the prying eyes of media savages.

"It's my fault," she confessed. "You just have to stay here in the room for a while. I promise this will all be over soon."

"Where will you be?" I said.

"I need to quench their thirst. Give them a recount of the entire timeline. I don't know. I'll figure it out." She drew a cloud from her arms.

"Hold on. What the hell am I going to do inside all by myself?" The panic of coming face to face with Saira threatened my sanity.

"Figure it out," she dismayed. "It'll be over soon. I promise." She was off to the main corridor. "Pray for her," she mouthed before turning away, stomping her heels on the lens-flashing herd.

"You can come visit now, sir." Nurse churned up a fresh smile after several minutes. Not enough time had passed to mellow my heart; however, the nurse's simple words piqued my interest. "She's lucky, you know, Saira. I wish everyone had a mother, friends like she does."

"Why do you say so? It must be common with all patients, though," I asked.

"There are people who come to visit because they must. Then there are people who come because they want to." She opened the dimly-lit patient room. For a second, the brick of depression fell hard on me. Saira had paled, barely human. She looked like a bone mat stitched in jute. *Did I somehow lead to all this?*

"She'll live again." Nurse's hands crinkled. "She has steel bones and a lot of well-wishers who just won't give up on her. Her mother just sits there. Every day. For hours. She reads her Gita. Shows her pictures. She's made of steel, too. Never cries, not in front of her." She paused, gesturing me to stoop, then she whispered. "But she cries."

Nurse was perhaps trying not to choke on her own words. "She cries a lot."

"You can sit right in, sir." The nurse enlarged her arms all the way to the chair. I had decided to call her Ms Torchbearer. She had lighted the path for me today.

"I'll give you some privacy." She closed the door.

I experienced the full lap of depressing solitary of the chlorine-smelling room in less than a minute since the nurse left. I wondered how Saira felt every moment of the last thirty days. Albeit in coma, she had gained the strength to move her one finger. In addition, she could see, listen, smell and cry.

"Hello, Saira," I said softly.

"Sorry to interrupt again." Ms Torchbearer barged right in. "If you don't mind, it'll take me a few minutes, but I need to clip her nails."

"Can you do it later?"

"I could. Definitely, I could. But, sir, she's already ripped a few bedsheets. I was supposed to do it before changing the sheets, but I didn't want you waiting any longer than you should." Her burger bite smile taped on her face again.

"Rip the sheets?"

"Ahm…" she stammered. "Let me show it instead." She dashed off, and in a jiffy, she was back. This time her arms came wrapped in linen. She flew the sheet up into the air and there it was, glaring hole in the shape of infinity.

"Why would she drill infinity?" I thought aloud.

"It isn't infinity, sir. It's the way she rips it, close to her hands." She turned the sheet upside down. I could see it bright and clear. *The number eight.* "I can get you other sheets, too. All twelve of them."

A slow creek ruptured Ria's hushed entry. "Hi angel," she said with joy to the nurse before skidding fast to me. "All the vultures are fed to their mouth." Her arms wrapped in mine cemented my courage and my respect for her. She had been doing the rounds in lieu of me, setting aside little quarrels, senseless arguments. She had trumped life above all else, and it was time I did the same.

Amaan

The night in the palace had turned celebratory to sparkling news from my hospital's visit today. Compassionate. Messiah. These were only a few of many adjectives flying on TV channels to describe me and Veer. For some it was complacent, but within me, a curious question refused to bow down. *What could Saira have meant by number eight?*

'Just leave it. What would you do if a finger was all you could move?' A wise voice echoed in my head, but my cat had decided to let the curiosity kill him through Google.

The first thing that came from the search was devil. *Is she possessed by the devil?* That was just weird. Even if she was possessed, then devil had a dumb way of scratching out of her body. It didn't make any sense.

I decided to move onto other stash of unraveled secrets of number eight. Fantasies, rituals, black magic, Hitler; this Google search had gone devil, too.

It was time to broom clues closer to home in lieu of googling the devils and Hitler. *Could it be the date she was hospitalized?* Nope, that wasn't eighth. *The time then?* That wasn't eight either.

"Are you ready for dinner?" Ria gently tapped in.

The dinner was surely up for a toss and so was the mystery of number eight was surely up for a toss.

Saira

A thundering sound of *eight angels and a pig* woke me up. From my bed, I could see outside the window. It was still dark. I couldn't figure out whether it was morning or evening. Hell, I didn't even know how I got here.

I leapt on the side table, took my fingers out, and peeled the drawers on the ground only to face the horrors of reality. *There was no phone. No watch. Nothing that was mine.*

The worst scenarios crossed my mind. *Am I kidnapped?*

I sprung to the window again. My only companion sat outside, atop that palm tree, the black and brown eagle, watching, and waiting. *Must be the prey that he seeks.* I was faraway, but I could see his claws digging with anger. He was mad, he was stuck. Just like me.

Another troupe of thunder woke me up again. When I woke up, I realized I couldn't remember how I fell asleep. I didn't know if I was asleep for minutes, hours, or days. *I've lived this day before, a sort of epiphany echoed in my ears.*

"Where am I?" I screamed, but all I heard back was my own voice. This was it, I decided. I tore off the bottom of my skirt, wrapped it on my arms, and went on with another scan of the walls until I hit the dents on the wall. I remembered etching through my nails, one mark for a day, and I had already counted thirty thus far.

Devoid of blankets or sheets, I once again lay on the floor, curled up to myself, my legs warming my stomach, my stomach heating my breasts.

"Enough," I shouted. I was going to crash and burn this place. First, I had to get out.

I tried jimmying the window, but a thought held my arms back. *Nope! Stay calm.* The worst of thoughts had begun snaking in already. I wasn't ready to accept it, not just yet. Maybe there's been a mistake. *Thirty days have gone by and I have not been assaulted.* At least there was no pain, no ache. I could walk well. I touched my breasts. They weren't sore either. Nothing felt broken. Not yet atleast.

"Are you sure about this?" A hush voice in the night choked me out of sleep. By now, I had learned my lesson. I didn't scream. I didn't even move an inch of my body. I just lay there, my eyes shut, my brain oiled with vigilance.

The hushed voice stopped.

Did I imagine it? It must be a nightmare, the one where monsters shifted shape, mouthed their dirty little desires, and touched wherever they felt like.

I stayed on the floor. Curled up. My ears rose like antlers, trying to find hooks in any conversation within my range. However, they returned empty.

"These are strange times and we don't have much of it." Finally, a different voice, a balmy male voice replied.

"Is there any other way?" The hushed voice appeared again, and this time it spoke from a face. *It was my mother.*

"Unfortunately, we don't." The balmy voice paused. "We have to use Eriksonian. We have to re-gut her." My spine frosted ice cold. *She wants to kill me!* "Think of it like the evolution," the balmy voice hissed.

"I don't understand any of this," my bitch mother had bubbles in her voice. *You'll pay for this one day. My death won't go unpunished.*

"Let me explain this to you. When survival is under threat, any specie, not just us humans, has only two options; either die or rise above the very toxins that threaten your existence.

"We'll create the toxins, just a bit more than her comfort. She'll resist first. Try to ignore it. She'll fight it with all her strength, too. Just when she thinks her arms are reaching the victory line, she'll lose."

"Will she feel any pain?" my mother asked.

"A bit. But the focus is too narrow. Part of her…"

"Shhh." A new voice hushed, shoving me into a tunnel filled with silence. *Shit, did they find me?* I flittered through my thrumming eyes, shuffling to find where these voices were coming from until my eyes flew over to the corner in the ceiling. There was a speaker tattooed in it. *Do they know that I can hear? I need to hide. Oh no, here they come.* I heard rapid footsteps, and to my reflex, I snuck back in many curls with my eyes wide shut and a heart galloping like a stallion.

"How could this have happened?" the balmy voice howled. "Get the plier." The speakers went dark again. This was it. My time to perish had come. I had only one wish; someone avenge my death from this balmy bastard and my bitch mother.

"You have to survive. Open your eyes!" The Pison slurped back to life in my blood. "Wake up and run. You have to survive." *I have to open my eyes.* "Wake up and run. I ain't done with you yet," Pison said.

I heard the thumping footsteps again. I could feel them breathing fire. "These must be the killers. Punch them left, right and center, use your legs too. What fucking difference does it make? You are dying anyway." Pison mocked me.

It was enough; it was time to fight back. I was ready to fight the killers. Here we go. Three, two, one, *go*!

"Hello, Saira!" It was the smiling face of Amaan. *I don't understand. I can't see well. I can't hear well.*

Saira

"Look at you, beautiful." Ria, I was certain, meant that. I would mean that, too, if I saw someone looking like me in my current pathetic state. My eyes buried in a dirty black swamp, my cheeks sucked like a plunger, my body hung like a shirt on a stick. Since my revival, I had only looked into the mirror once, and I was determined not to look in it again, not until I gathered all my spunk.

"You're a survivor," she said. "Not many survive a plunge into death for three months."

That was the first time it dawned that I had been dead for three months. Coma, to be medically accurate.

"Hey. Look at you!" Amaan walked right in alongside my mother.

"Hi, my baby!" My mother and I dissolved in a hug. I knew she was there by me the whole time. She cared, but there was also a growing sense of déjà vu that something was not right, not with her, not with me; but her and me together.

"You have to thank god for giving you a mother like her," Amaan professed. "She put her life on hold for you."

"It was her idea to put that documentary tape," Amaan mentioned.

"I'd rather not talk about it," I murmured.

"It's okay, Saira." Amaan smiled.

"They got the guy who leaked it online," Mrs Gaina was quick to respond. "Almost. But everyone knows it wasn't you!"

"What do you mean?" Amaan asked the same question.

"You didn't know?" Mrs Gaina questioned. "We sent a full report to the palace last week."

"Report from who?"

"The private investigation."

"Yes." Amaan nodded. "Of course. That's the one you're talking about."

"All that's behind us now," Ria responded.

"How did the show go?" I changed the topic, hoping to cheer everyone in the room, especially me.

"The documentary was a super hit," Amaan responded. "But obviously not because of anything scandalous."

"That's good then." I heaved a sigh of relief.

"Yes it is. You're famous now," he added. "They made the show as much about my mother as about you."

"I don't understand?"

"A courageous woman documenting another courageous woman."

"I'm glad all the misconceptions were sorted."

"Don't worry about it," my mother assured. "Tell me this. Are you ready to go home?"

I didn't want to go back to that home. *What if the attacker came back?* That fear had left all its footprints on my face.

"Don't worry, baby. We're not going to Attanooga. It's a much warmer place and it has a palm tree." That made me feel worse. Much worse. I wanted to throw up, and I did. *Oh gosh, what did I do? I was supposed to be beautiful. Not be tied to a puke-filled hospital bed. There wasn't much left to salvage my persona, was it?*

Amaan

"What just happened to Saira?" Mrs Gaina was flustered. We all were. Just when we thought the ropes were getting tighter, the wind drenched the boat back in the water.

"She had an epileptic attack," the doctor murmured. "She's fine now, but we'll get our specialist Dr Kaar to see her first thing tomorrow morning."

"No. It's okay," Mrs Gaina resisted. "Years ago, she got treatment from this place, Nesting, and I'd like to take her there."

"As you wish," doctor complied. "Is the place close by?"

"It's in Kerala, by the coast."

"I'd not suggest moving her till she's in ICU," the doctor said.

"It's going to be okay, Mrs Gaina," Ria said. "Please let Amaan and me know if there's anything we could do."

"Wait a minute," I blurted. The name *Kaar* was too unique a family name and too familiar. "Is this Roneet Kaar you're talking about, doctor?"

He admitted that it was indeed the same person.

"I know him!" I exclaimed, much to Ria's blindness. "We can definitely have Ron take a look at Saira!" I was trying to secure Mrs Gaina's doubts.

"Who's Ron?" Ria questioned with an unpredictable cynicism.

"We went to med school together. We call him Ron. You know, short for Roneet. He can help with these incidents. At least narrow down the triggers. So she could prevent its occurrence in future and recover faster should the symptoms arise."

"I still can't believe that she hurt herself." Mrs Gaina had de-mummified the incident once again, along with its hooks and misery. "I'm scared for her," she whimpered.

"You mentioned she's been getting treatment?" I asked. "Could the epilepsy be relates to that?"

"That was depression. Just once." A lacuna ensued. "She never had epileptic attacks, ever," she said.

"She's suffered like none of us can fathom." A ravine of affection poured through Ria's eyes. "Please let us know once you've made your decision. It could be Amaan's friend doctor or the one you choose. You are her mother. You know what's best for her." Her smile unfurled with remarkable plastic.

Ria's words were kind, but I'd sensed her ill intentions. It felt like something disturbing was lurking in the air around us. I knew that feeling too well. I felt like a stranded man on a highway as all the cars sped by.

"We'll leave now, Amaan?" Ria moved forward, ready to haul out of this place.

"Let's just make a decision quickly," I declared, much to Ria's discontent. I had avowed that I wouldn't use someone else's pen to write my diary. Not since my father tried the same trick. "Saira isn't in the best shape, and we shouldn't delay, considering the unpredictability of her symptoms," I appealed to Mrs Gaina.

"I do have to rush for a meeting." Ria threw the ball right back, hitting me hard in the ribs. "Good luck, Mrs Gaina, and I'll see you later, Amaan." Her belligerence squeezed my courage, but more than that, it was the shock, as if she was in someone else's skin.

Mrs Gaina must have felt the heat, too. "I think we can have Ron look at her while she gains strength, then we can take her to Nesting, the specialized care facility."

I felt like good bones. My reckoning had come. I wasn't a demented, weak child whom my father always thought me to be. I was capable of taking hard stands. I'll deal with Ria, but innocent lives came first, even if it was a once-friend-now-stranger's life.

Amaan

"Can you do me one last favour?" Saira asked before rolling in the space-ship-like observatory of Ron's special section in the hospital building.

"Sure," I replied.

"Until I recover, and that is only until then—" she stopped.

"What is it?"

"Forget about it," she murmured.

"C'mon, Saira. We have decades of camaraderie. Don't let a few stale moments take all that away."

"It's not you." She paused. "It's just, never mind."

"You have to tell me, for the sake of good times we spent together."

She inhaled a pool of gas. "Until I recover, would it be okay if I stay in touch with you?"

"Of course," I said. "Why would you even ask? I'm here already."

"I don't want to cause any strains between you and Ria."

"Don't worry. It'll take a lot to scrape me off her." I smiled.

"And thank you for finding a reason for my mother to not be here." I agreed, but I was also confused, not knowing why a daughter would do that to her own mother, the one who stood right beside her day and night for months until she gained consciousness.

"You must be wondering why?" She plucked the words right out of their tissue. "I wish I could tell you." She sobbed. "I wish I knew..." Her hands on her face couldn't stop the drips. "I'm not a monster. But I just can't. Not just yet."

My hands skirted onto hers; perhaps a touch was needed to bring water of different colors together.

"Any family with her?" Ron asked, multitasking through a wall of monitors lined up in two rows, the bottom five to showcase the results of biosensors, the top five to view the stream of five cameras within the observatory room.

"Her mother. I asked her to rest. She's been through hell in these past months, and her blood pressure was acting up." I felt proud of the empathy I was creating along the way.

"It's just you then. Trying to fix your girlfriend. What a noble gesture."

"She isn't my girlfriend." I coughed my denial.

"Her name is Saira, correct?"

"Yes."

"I'm pretty sure you mentioned her to me back in the U.S. A lot."

"Can we just focus on her tests, please?"

"Yes, for now. We have a lot of catching up to do. You left med school, then poof! You just vanished?"

"We certainly have a lot of catching up to do." I signalled Ron to look ahead, as Saira's bed rolled in from the backdoor and stationed right in the middle of the room. Wire creepers emerged and latched onto her arms, her temples, her legs, and even under her hair.

"Don't' worry. It's going to be okay. You need to take your mind off this." Ron's tap was comforting.

She had barely recovered and, here she was, a rat in a lab. Maybe Ria was right all along.

Thoughts of Ria flourished the dried branch of friction back in me, I was certain I was going to have a day in court just for the amiss of hiding this from her. *There you go, now I was mad at myself. Not just for this. I insulted Saira, demeaned her, and for what? She didn't do anything wrong. How could this get any worse?*

The clock circled through many cups of coffee. The slow REM phase had started a while back. There was no movement yet. Saira slept like a baby. It's beside the point that Ron had doped her with enough sleeping pills. It was the peace on her face, it suited her. She needed it.

"Amaan!" A shrill of a sound alerted me.

It felt like a child calling my name. The observation deck was bright white, and there she was, calmly walking towards the one-sided mirror. She couldn't see me, but she could see her own reflection. Even though paled, she looked beautiful.

After our indiscretion at the fort, I recalled looking at her for hours until she woke up. I could feel the dirty layers of the past eroding away, stitching all my tissues in peace. I hoped she felt the same calmness as I did, but she didn't.

Her own reflection rattled her. She moved backwards, slowly at first, and then charged like a bull. *How could one run backwards?*

I realized she saw the door in the mirror; she knew it was a reflection. It was a hint. Her mind was alert!

A juxtaposed anomaly to the amount of drugs in her system. The ripples flared, as she gunned for the door. Before she'd clasp on to the door knob, she tripped on the turn stairs, falling flat under her own dress, screaming in pain, screaming for help, scrambling to get her head out of her dress, and when she did get her face out, those eyes, that face. *This wasn't the Saira I knew.*

"Stop it! You can't go in there," Ron blasted. The nurse didn't even flinch, her eyes squarely beamed on the computer monitors, glaring at the spaghetti lines rolling from all the sensors on Saira, but I think there was something in those readings that gravitated her well-spread brows closer, almost inseparable.

"Screw you!" I dashed to the door. "I can't let this happen."

"It's your choice, Amaan. However, this won't be of any help if we pull her out right now.

"She's on a lot of sedatives that are not good for her body, and you really want her to go through the cycle again?" I didn't know what to do, and this wouldn't be the first time I wasn't ready to make a decision. Perhaps that's what made me madder.

"You know the room is padded. She can't hurt herself." Ron breathed softly. "Here you go, drink this water, and you can wait outside." He paused. "You don't have to be here."

I sunk in the chair. My mind was so blank that I could hear every drop of water going down my esophagus. They say it only happens when you're about to die.

Amaan

"I have good news and not-so good news, Amaan," Ron announced.

"Let's lay it all out," I said. Seven days had passed since Saira's tests.

"Okay. You remember the first thing she did during observation?" Ron asked.

"She woke up and walked, and then she curled in a corner."

"That's right. She walked. Therefore, the first reaction was a motor action, not a behavioral one. It all sounds bad, but here's the silver line." That second long pause felt like a lifetime. "I can say with 95% accuracy that she isn't suffering from schizophrenia."

"That's a relief!" I wished that disease for no one and never for Saira. *So young and so full of life.*

"She's fine. There's no paranoia. None in her history. If it was you, I'd be doubtful, though." I enjoyed Ron's joke this time. "Seriously, though, her vitals, psychiatry report, and all observations confirm that. However, she does suffer from somnambulism."

"What's that?"

"The more common term is sleepwalking."

"Sleepwalking?" It felt so common a term that it wasn't even a disease in my mind.

"See, there are three types of sleepwalking. Arousal Sleep Disorder, Nocturnal Frontal Lobe Disorder and the REM disorder. Of these three, the latter two are associated with early stages of grave diseases. Nocturnal Frontal Lobe Disorder aligns with epilepsy and REM aligns with Parkinson's."

"So she has the nocturnal one?"

"We aren't sure. Her prognosis is more towards arousal sleep disorder. There isn't a single epileptic incident before the one she suffered while in ICU. I'd like to observe her more before squeezing her into the nocturnal frontal lobe category.

"We must give her the benefit of doubt. She suffered a traumatic event with three months in coma."

Ron played the first video of observation. "Look here!" I didn't want to look at those videos, period.

Her eyes opened lazily, then slowly she stepped out of the bed, and without putting her slippers on, she walked. The slow walk bloomed brisk in no time, and she began to walk rapidly backward toward the door, not realizing that the door was three steps down. She stumbled and fell.

"Okay, that's it." I paused the video myself.

Ron swiveled away from the TV and so did his stare. "This is the first day, and after we ruled out schizophrenia, I watched these tapes again. Initially I thought her severity of sleepwalking was critical. See, generally in sleepwalking people are aware of life-threatening or life-harming hurdles such as stairs. Often you'll see that sleepwalkers will roam around and stop at stairs, and most often when they encounter such a hurdle, they come back to bed and sleep."

"But she jumped right off those steps?" I asked.

"She did. But only that day." Ron quickly browsed to other files on his big TV screen and played the next one, and the one after next, and the one after. "See here?"

I could see, and I didn't have to be half-a-doctor to know what Ron was about to say. "She backed off the stairs every time except for that first time."

"Did we alter the sedatives, anything changed in subsequent sessions?" I asked.

"Nope."

"Some trigger makes it worse then?"

"You got it. If I had to guess, there was some door left open the night she jumped off the second floor, or the time when she got the epileptic attack."

Ron continued. "Now, if I were you, I'd focus on the other days and try to keep the routine, the stress on same level as the other days, when her pattern was normal."

He paused before adding, "It's indeed difficult to find the trigger."

"But if we do find it, her condition will go away forever?" I was curious.

"Possibly." Ron spoke after a drilling breath. "And now the not-so-good news." He rewound the tapes and zoomed in on Saira's mouth. "You see that?" he asked.

I could see her murmur. "Yes. She's whispering something," I acknowledged.

"That's right. But it's the *what* she's whispering that startled me," he said. "If you look closely, you'll notice that she isn't whispering. She's reciting, like we recite prayers when we're gripped with fear."

"So she thinks she's in danger?"

"Could be. But look at her body language." Saira's hands curled under her thighs, her eyes wary of everything around her. She wasn't in danger. She was hiding something.

"What is she hiding?"

"That's a good question. And I don't think you can get that answer easily," Ron said.

"Why?"

"Because it's protected information, and, whatever she is reciting is connected to it."

"You mean like hypnotherapy?"

"Yes."

"And?"

"I can try to unlock it, but without knowing the whole history, it could become risky for her. Her incidents of sleepwalking might increase and she might drift toward schizophrenia too."

"That's horrible."

"These are all theoretical risks. The question is, are we willing to take that chance on Saira? She's so young, and she has her whole life ahead of her."

Ron was right. "What does that leave us with?" I asked.

"There's one way to end this for good." Ron's plan swam with a furious speed. It was dangerous, but then I looked at the screen again. This time I picked up Saira's fingers. She wasn't just drawing eight on the floor. It was a familiar poem "Eight angels and a pig… eight angels and a pig…"

Amaan

"Your phone is stubborn." Saira had noticed the relentless buzz, which wasn't quite the focus for me. With me, I had a barrel of bad news, and I had to find a way to relay it without being the bad news bearer.

"Oh. That's just my phone on its Roomba class," I said.

"I meant your phone is vibrating."

"I get it. I was just saying that the phone is not vibrating. It's attending a Roomba class."

"That doesn't make any sense," she said.

"I know. I was trying to be funny." I paused. "Apparently not." Perhaps it was the pity on me, which made her smile. I couldn't say if she was happy or not, but she definitely wasn't claw hammered by her sufferings.

"So here's the thing, Saira. I have good news and bad news. What do you want to hear first?" I was doing my best to hide all the jitters under a pebble stone.

"Nothing is going to surprise me anymore. If the bad news says I have a tumor or cancer, then let's start with the good one first. We can drown in the sorrows thereafter."

"Now I have double good news, then!" I exclaimed.

"If it keeps going at this pace, who knows, I might become human again."

"So, you don't have cancer and..." I paused. Perhaps I shouldn't have, but before I realized that.

"So I have tumour," she murmured.

"You don't have tumor, too!" I said quickly.

She sighed heavily before unleashing the aftermath. "You need to work on your bedside manners."

"I know," I said, bringing a second cheer onto her face.

"Now I'm going to tell you to not pick up that call," she announced at the dawn of another round of incessant buzz. "You need to reveal the killer first."

"Second good news. As established by the other doctors, your scars are consistent with that of a natural fall or accidental scarring. In other words, there was no other party or intruder involved that night."

"How did I get hurt then?"

"You have a common condition called sleepwalking, and some idiot left the door open that night. You wandered into the balcony and fell onto the bushes. Thank god it wasn't a pavement or concrete."

"I'll never be safe then," she bemoaned, as if coating a new form of hostile truth around her life.

"It's a pretty common condition, and there are tons of ways to avoid it," I said. "I don't think you should be worried about it."

"But it happened, right?" she hissed.

"There are precautions you can take to control it."

"What precautions?"

There's a whole ritual. Which starts with me sleeping naked next to you… I had no idea why these crazy stupid jokes were coming to my mind, but I had the sanity to block them at the gate. "We need to identify stressors, and then find a way to stop them from detonating."

"And what happens when the stressors get detonated?"

"First thing first, it can be avoided. Second, even if it's triggered, we can take precautions for it to not be life-threatening. You know, like locking the doors, cleaning the kitchen of any utensils."

"Utensils? You mean knives?" Her face turned into a squeeze ball, drained, then puffed again.

"Listen, this is the first incident. Something drastic must have happened to trigger it. What happened that day?"

"Nothing," she said flatly.

"You don't remember?"

She just wobbled her head. I couldn't tell if she didn't remember or she didn't want to tell me. Either way, it wasn't my place to ask. "And there's one more thing."

"What?"

"Do you have any memory of seeing a hypnotherapist?"

"No. I don't," she replied. "Why do you ask?"

"Because Ron said that it will be a good idea to have you see your therapist again, if you've had one before."

"Nope. Thankfully never been through that." She laughed.

I was wondering if I should mention to her what Ron had told me. Her carving of eight on the sheets, her recital of eight angels and a pig? It all looked like tiny Lego pieces of a giant puzzle, and its mystery sucked me right in. I didn't feel like ruining her time with yet another stressor. "Good then!" I said.

"But why did you ask about the therapist?"

"It's always a good idea to go see your therapist in coma recovery phase. That's it. No big deal!"

"I don't need any therapist." She smiled again. "I need to get out into the world," she said, her lips pressed, her dimple perfectly welled, and her mind at ease. This was her well-deserved peace, and I didn't intend to snatch it away.

"Take rest. If you need anything, press the button by the nightstand," I said.

"Thank you for everything. For the doctor. For letting me stay in your Delhi house."

"Not a big deal." I reveled in my accomplishment.

I had finally become the man my mom always wanted me to be and it was in my own way, not the way my father wanted.

Unfortunately, not the way Ria wanted it right now, too. It was time to step out of the room and have a conversation with her. The one I had been avoiding for a few days and at least a dozen missed calls just today.

Amaan

"I think we need to talk." Ria's frozen words rocked down the phone. For the first time, I heard Ria like never before.

"What's up?" I greeted.

"Where are you?" she asked.

"In the Delhi house."

"Are you alone?"

"Saira is resting here too."

"What do you think is going on?"

"Nothing. It's fine. She just got discharged, so she'll be here for a couple of days, but I'm coming to you."

"You allowed her in our bedroom?"

"Not our bedroom. The guest room."

"You're missing the point, Amaan. I'm more than supportive and I feel for Saira and her conditions. But…" She trespassed through the blunt road.

Here came the unleashing of *but*. "It can't be affecting our relationship. You've been gone for almost a week now. We've hardly seen each other, and you are cozying up with her."

"I know I owe you a review of the new terms for the hotel deal," I carved out a different road.

"Screw hotel. I don't care about the hotel!" She raised her voice. The first time I ever heard that. "I'm talking about us."

"What about us? What's wrong with that?"

"You don't think there's anything wrong with us?" Her sarcasm hit me hard.

"Is that why you didn't tell me about the investigation report clearing Saira?" I galloped on a different hill.

"Don't change the topic."

"I'm not. This is relevant to our conversation right now."

"I forgot about it, or I didn't think it was that important. Quite honestly, I don't even remember it."

"Really?" I paused. "Are we going to do that now?"

She stayed mum, and then spoke. "But, it's true. I don't like her in our lives."

"Relax. She'll never be in a position to do that," I replied. "You have to see the videos of those tests. She could be on the verge of losing it."

"And you could be on the verge of losing me." That was a bit abrupt.

"What's wrong with you? You were the one who blabbered that I shouldn't abandon her, that I should take care of her."

"And I'm the one telling you to move away from her."

"That'd be a bit rude. Wouldn't it?"

"She has her mother to take care of her. And you're just inserting yourself into the situation."

"I'm not inserting myself. Saira needs my help."

"Saira needs help. She didn't ask for your help."

"You don't know half the story then."

"Enlighten me."

"Okay. So, Saira thinks that her mother," I paused. I felt hesitant to say anything further.

"That her mother is evil?"

"Not exactly evil... how do you know this anyway?"

"We went to the same college. That's been the story of her life. Her mother is an evil person, and she's the damsel in distress turned rebel."

"You're patronizing."

"No, I am not." She flared down a bit. "See, I don't wish anyone to go through what she went through, but now she's coming back to normalcy, and she has her mother to take care of her. All I'm saying is that there are other things that you need to focus on."

If what Ria said about Saira's sob story was true, it pissed me off, but I couldn't ignore what Ron had said, too.

"How about this?" I tried to infuse color in Ria's tone, but it remained cold as a brick of ice. "I won't call her. Promise."

"And if you do, I'll walk away. I promise," Ria muttered, then walked away from the call. Literally. Leaving me swirling down a trench of my own.

Three Months Later

Amaan

"It's the same place as in my nightmare, Amaan. I see myself locked in a hospital with a palm tree upfront and a dramatic background score of *eight angels and a pig*," I recalled Saira's plea to avoid this hospital in the first place, as I drawled in the sprawling verandah of the Nesting facility, overlooking the wet sand leading up to Arabian Sea.

"You think she'll be okay now?" I raised my guilt to Mrs Gaina, who sat stiff on a wicker chair. All she could spare was an orphan eye. She wasn't stoic or the iron clad monster Saira had made out of her. She sat there, seemingly confused, disappointed, perhaps like any mother with a fractured relationship with her only child.

"I want you to know that Saira didn't want to come here," I said.

She stepped into sunlight. The paleness on her face was staggering, as if she had suddenly aged many decades in this moment. "You're a nice boy, Amaan. You always have been. Even ten years ago. I remember on one Valentine's Day you had come to our house and asked for Saira's hand. You were ready to marry her. You really loved her. I could see that in your eyes," she paused. "I still see it in your eyes." Her voice was straight as a scale.

"I'm sorry?" I was bewildered.

"You can't hide your love for Saira in your eyes."

"I think you're mistaken, Mrs Gaina. I've broken all strings with her. You know all that."

"Does Ria know you are here?" she asked.

I didn't want to answer her. Not at all. I loved Ria. I had to pull myself out of this mess, once and for all. "I feel guilty if I gave that impression," I said. "And if you think that way, I can only imagine what Saira must feel like."

She turned to me with a smile dipped in scepticism. "I've had many failed relationships in my life, and Saira seems to have picked up on that gene, too. I always managed to move on, and so did she."

"There's absolutely nothing going on." My breath swelled.

"I'm here because Saira requested me to, and Ron agrees that it'll be good for her. That's all. I'm just trying to finish what I started. There's nothing more to it. And if this is your way to have me pull out of her life, then so be it. One thing is quite clear, though, that you've never been a fan of hers."

"No, I haven't," she confessed. "But that doesn't mean I don't love her." Her words were acidic.

"You sure have a unique way of showing your love then."

"You'll understand it one day. What all we must do to protect our loved ones." Her rosettes darkened with her faux smile.

"I don't know what you did to her. But nothing can take her back to that time." I was still pissed at the charade of injecting politics into an innocent friendship between me and Saira. It was a reprieve that this ordeal was on a short runway. The sooner Saira was re-stitched, the faster I'd tow myself out of her swamp.

"That was the whole point." Her smile weakened. "Saira's mind isn't the best. I think we both can agree on that."

I didn't want to agree on anything with her. It was evident why Saira was so mad with her all the time. Thus far, she had nothing nice to say about her.

"In fact, the reason we went for hypnosis was to provide clarity in her mind. To have her focus on the right things," she continued.

"And how has that worked out for you?" My entire nicety had cut ties with her.

"Quite good, actually." She remained oblivious to my untoward overtures.

"You have a pretty lose definition of good, don't you?" Her inert smile climbed back up."You did what you thought was best. Now let's do what's best for Saira," I said.

"Isn't what we're doing?"

"Yes. What I meant was that Ron has already shared his prognosis with this hospital. And now we need to get Saira back to how she was."

"That's what you want, don't you?" Kindness had slid out of her trousers.

"This is your daughter, Mrs Gaina," I said. "Don't make this about me."

"I'm not making it about you. You are." This was the first I had seen the heinous phantom of Mrs Gaina.

"How so?" I was defiant.

"You want her to be like she was when you guys were in love," she barked.

I detected the bubbles of my boiling blood, only if I could squirt them out in spite. "You're quite delusional, Mrs Gaina." Instead, I led the assault with my words.

"Apparently not for the rest of your family." She was in no mood for diplomacy today. I couldn't say anything to it. I had to concede. "All I want to say is that if we do what you're suggesting, I want you to know that it will be a messy state." She aimed the rifle straight at me.

"This would be sad if it wasn't funny." I paused. "This is the first I've heard of such grave dangers of hypnosis!"

"It isn't hypnosis." Her muffled feelings leaked out of her words. "It's her."

"You talk like she's killed someone."

"No. Not her." Her words slashed her tongue.

"She's an adult now. Whatever childhood attention-deficit disorder she had, she can deal with it. At least she wouldn't be living in fear of her own shadow, her own sleep, her own body." She remained tranquil in her whistling breath."You need to let her be an adult now. Just let go," I implored.

"I won't be able to, unfortunately," she said as her feet rustled before pouncing toward me, which meant she had something direct to ask me. "Then see to it that she gets a fair treatment. Just the way she wants it."

"Why do you need me to do this?"

"Because no one gets her trust, but for some reason you have."

I listened to every word, nodded, affirmed, but there was a strange sense that something malicious was baking under the surface that I had barely scratched. One thing was sure; Mrs Gaina was not to be trusted.

Saira

The palm tree still hung on the window. The eagle hadn't aged a day. Paint doesn't age, nor does the evil that was still roosting in the place. I felt like I'd been enchanted again, stripped of all my ammunition, and then shoved into a matchbox. Only, I wasn't allowed to be lit up.

Footsteps on the door turned my attention to the two beacons in my life. One full of dark flames, the other a string of lights irradiating my soul.

"Hi, Saira," Amaan greeted.

I didn't nod when he jabbered *Hi, Saira*. I was mad. "So now you're complicit with my dear mommy, aren't you?" I said.

"An ocean apart from it."

"Just one?"

"Wait till evening." His sense of humor wasn't lost on me anymore. I wanted to hate him for tricking me into getting in this place. Instead, I just lost all my angry feathers. In its stead, I was roiling up with adrenaline. I had no idea why.

"So it looks like you'll be out of this place by tomorrow," Amaan expanded.

"How do you know?"

"Doctor said so."

"You have to go through another procedure," Amaan interrupted.

"What procedure?" This was the first I heard of a goddamn procedure.

The room suddenly transformed into a congregation of silent moments, and it had begun to freak me out. "Someone say something? My dear mother?"

"For once, don't blame me." Her head swiveled to Amaan.

"I don't know how not to lay it out there. So here it is." Amaan had begun to unshackle his throat. "Dr Guha, the doctor that worked on you before, will undo whatever he did to fix you of your issues, and then he'll patch it back up."

"You mean he'll operate on me?"

"No. Not at all." Amaan's quick denial was a relief.

"He'll bring to surface whatever it is that he suppressed with hypnosis ten years ago."

I was swallowed in a giant sink hole right from under my feet. "Is this some sort of a joke?"Amaan looked up to me in a failed bid to pass on some sympathy. "What did he do to me ten years ago?" My eyes were now darted on my mother.

She was reluctant at first, but easily persuaded back in line. "You had some trouble focusing in school days, and Dr Guha fixed it with hypnosis."

"And you hid it from me?"

"That happened when you were a child. It wasn't all that important; besides, doctor said it's best to let you grow up normally," she cautioned, even though mildly, but that's all I needed to explode.

"How dare you have the guts to do something like that to me?" I roared. "You're the most pathetic piece of shit mother in this whole goddamn earth."

The humiliation surfaced on her face. All over her mascara. My words didn't sting her; I am sure it was Amaan's presence. I was sure she wanted to bang him. Maybe I should tell her that, but I decided to eat the hate instead, only out of respect for Amaan.

"C'mon, Saira," Amaan interrupted. *Why is his tone condescending?* "I don't want to insert myself into this, obviously, but I have to tell you that your mom was by your side, day in and day out."

"You don't know her, Amaan." He had to know the reality. "This is what she does. She makes my life a mess, then cleans up just so that she comes out as the messiah who saved her little spoilt daughter."

She still stayed mum. *Trying to be the martyr. Oh, so now she has a new strategy. What a grade-A-extra-large bitch.*

"I'm leaving," my mother announced.

"Go. Already," I yelled. "A decade later, but, hey, it's better than never."

"Sorry, Amaan. This is your problem now," she said in such a pretentious little tone.

"Mrs Gaina. What are we doing here?" Amaan interjected.

"We're leaving too." I announced.

"But it's important to have at least one session with Dr Guha, and he isn't back until tomorrow." Amaan was unnecessarily worried.

"I'm fine."

"You clearly are fine in some way and may not be in some others." Amaan's rude comments threw a blanket of ice-cold silence. I figured it was my turn to thaw the block of ice.

"I can see any doctor as long as she isn't here," I announced.

"There you go." My mother was so decisive.

"It's my choice." I was irritated. "You don't get to make that decision or bless it with your 'there you go'."

"Okay, Saira." She was out of the door, almost. I had a feeling she wanted to have the last word. "I'll sign you as the official legal guardian now, Amaan. The glory is all yours now!"

Moments later, armed with a signed letter, she dashed back. "Amaan, will you please sign it?"

Amaan stood and read the content of the letter to his satisfaction. "Are you sure?" he asked.

"Like you said, it's about time I treat Saira like an adult." My mother's tone wasn't bitter, but I bet her thoughts were.

"I can manage it all myself. I'm not a kid."

"No, you're not," Amaan announced. "I'll be with you, and then we'll get you discharged tomorrow." He signed the letter.

My mother fled out of the room like a guava fleeing a parrot bite. *She had finally left me!* I felt like a girl on the beach, and I wasn't there to have fun, but really just to bury my face in the sand.

How could I face Amaan after my embarrassing outbreak?

"I get your frustration," he said. His warm touch had the magic of eucalyptus oil, rubbing away all the stress with his infusing shoulder massage. "Your mom can be a bit tough. But let's try to forget the last few moments of our lives and focus on getting you out of this place, shall we?"

I felt protected after a long time. I was finally safe. I wanted the feeling to last forever. *Why did you leave me ten years ago, Amaan? I loved you then. I love you now. I need you. I'm for you. I was so stupid that I tried to damage our relationship over some stupid story. What is wrong with me?*

"Are you sure you can handle the psycho Saira? Well now, even I don't know what or who I am?" I quickly dissed the romance out of my thoughts.

"So let me tell you a little about the hypnotherapy." He clutched my hands, as if to drain my fears. "It's a common practice worldwide to get rid of bad habits, like for children with attention-deficit disorder."

"Okay, so you also think I'm a nut case!"

"Stop it,"Amaan gushed.

"Seriously, though. I am a bit scared, Amaan."

"I know," he said, then he stood to walk out.

"Are you leaving me, too?"

"Yes, to get a toothbrush from the hotel. I guess I'll be the guardian on the couch today."

"I can't wait until tomorrow! We get to find out how you used to jump around in school with your attention-deficit disorder," Amaan said.

"And you're going to do that looking like this monkey?" I playfully pointed to his cargo shorts and polo t-shirt.

"Why. What's wrong in this?"

"I have generally seen more of a mini mouse night suit."

"Really? I am sleeping on a couch for you and I get this? There's no place for a good deed on this planet." He smirked.

"I'm just messing with you."

"Good night!" His words cracked a genuine smile on him.

"Good night," I replied, returning the room to the darkness that I still remembered from many years ago.

"Hey, do you mind if I turn on one light?" I appealed.

"Sure. What happened?" he quipped. "You okay?"

I couldn't tell him how scared I was. I was like a kid who had seen her soccer ball fly into the basement, then told to spend the night in darkness there. I didn't want to sleep. I feared, what if I slept and not be able to wake up again. So instead, I blurted, "It's just a temporary adjustment phase. Doctor tells me it will go away in a few months."

He listened earnestly. I could tell he wasn't pretending.

His words came lathered in solace. "I can only imagine what you've gone through." He questioned then. "Is it true what they say? That it's like a rebirth?"

"I don't know what rebirth looks like. The last memory is pretty far away from my birthday suit!"

He chuckled. It was nice to see him relaxed.

I continued, "This whole incident has changed me a bit. You know what I see when I look into the mirror? I don't see a girl with ambition; I don't see a girl with desire. I see a girl with life." Amaan pulled up closer; the valley between our beds remained full of lull.

I had to confess to him. He didn't deserve the heartache I caused him. Therefore, I professed, "I should have kept you informed of everything that was going on with that story."

He stayed quiet.

"So what if my channel played me, I should have protected you. Nothing was so staggering that I couldn't tackle, but then I ended up screwing up the only real relationship. The one I keep boomeranging to."

"That tree is cut, woods burned, and now a new tree stands in its place." He smiled. "Tomorrow you'll be a brand new person. Maybe tomorrow you'll have an answer to every puzzle from last decade."

"I don't care about my past. I just want to live in the present. I don't wish the relationship I have with my mother on anyone. I do want you to know that all I have is admiration for Queen Sana and I wish I had a mother like her."

"Well. That would be odd," he replied.

"Why?"

"We've dated and have hooked up together."

"Whatever. Look at me now… so undesirable," I said.

"I have to be honest. You looked like a zombie, not to say skinny girls aren't pretty, but not my type."

"Thanks for your cynical consolation."

"I didn't finish. Look at you now. In six short weeks, you are better than ever. The glow on your skin… I am afraid it's going to blind me, dear."

I couldn't help but blush. He continued, "And that smile; those eyes; look at that slippery body."

His compliments shone my soul. No one had complimented me in a while. Not with such fun anyway. We looked at each other in a way we had done before, where there were no covers, no masks, just us, naked in our mind, naked in our body, but full of each other in our souls.

"You can come sleep on the bed. The couch will give Your Highness a backache, and then I'll get blamed for that."

"I'm having a backache already." Those mischievous eyes stood out.

"I can massage it, if you like."

"That will be some extraordinary exploitation. In a hospital, in a patient room… having the patient massage me!"

We wore our smiles back. "You're right. You should massage me instead!" I simpered.

"I don't mind that."

"I don't mind that either." I maintained my calm. My heart, however, ran like a starving wolf. My face hid under my smile. I wanted to keep smiling. I wanted to be happy like this forever, and it mutated when the road between us disappeared, only the breaths remained, rest of us had become one.

I lay face down, the threads of my hospital gown loosened, my bare back all for him. I could feel him sitting on my hips, gently stroking me as his hands slipped up and down from my neck to my waist, climbing up my hips, but just stopping short, and then sliding up again; this time he made a fancy detour.

Saira

Everything about Dr Guha's office was creepy. There was no observatory deck. There were no cameras. This wasn't a doctor's office; this was a fuck shack. The lounge chaise lay there in the middle, soiled in a litre of bodily fluids.

"Hi, Saira." The voice came to the foreground, the footsteps stopped.

I turned, and for a moment, it seemed that all the pieces of my theory reshuffled out of order. None of the Legos matched. This wasn't what I had expected, not at all.

"Thank you, Gowri." Dr Guha asked his attendant to leave. "I can take it from here." He rolled his wheelchair and locked it in his spot, right next to the chaise. "So, Saira. I see that Prince Amaan has signed off as your guardian."

"Yes."

"Is he outside?"

What does he want? Me to tell him my secrets? I guessed this pervert saw a video of Amaan and me last night. He probably already knew that Amaan wasn't here. He probably also knew where he was headed.

"No," I crowed.

"Should I call your mother?"

"No."

"What can I do to get an answer that isn't no?"

"What do you need them for?"

"Just a protocol."

"Amaan will be back soon."

"Very well then. Let's talk about you. You're all grown up." He gently waved at me to come sit at the chaise. My head drained. Not even a single thought passed by, sans a déjà vu, like *this had happened before*.

"We've met before. Haven't we?" I asked.

"Nothing as exotic or sinful as you must be imagining right now, but yes, we have. Several times."

"Was it around the time I missed a school year?"

"Possibly."

"How long was I here?"

"A while."

"Why was I here?"

"We'll get to all your questions… and answers."

This man was nothing like the sleazy monster I had imagined. A distant memory of meeting him marched forward. In which he looked much different.

"When did you have this accident?"

"You mean this wheelchair? This I've had for as long as I can remember."

"If you don't mind me asking, how?"

"I was born with this condition." He paused. "I was born much worse actually. I couldn't do anything myself. My sisters and my mother took care of me."

"What about your father?"

"He left us." Moments later, he picked up again. "That's quite common actually."

"No, it's not. That's horrible."

"Oh, don't get me wrong. That's horrible, yes. But that's common, too. My father, for example, didn't need a doctor; he had this self-healing ability to forget bad things that were around him." Dr Guha chuckled.

I didn't find it funny. His father was an absolute animal. The one who should've been punished.

"He was a monster," I declared.

"Aren't we all?" he replied. "In someone's eyes."

I was dragged by my feet and thrown straight into the guilt tub. I had been imagining monstrous intents, quite contrary to him being this admirable fighter. Much like me.

"Then how did you fix yourself?" I asked.

He inflated a long wide circle of breath, and then continued, "Self-determination and by helping others. I had to turn whatever was left in me to strength, and then once I tried it on myself and got some success, I decided it was safe to use my method to heal the world."

"And you opened this?" My arms flew apart, dwarfing his entire hospital in it.

"Yes. One hundred percent guilty of that." His calm face clipped a tiny smile.

"How come there are no pictures of you around here?" My journalistic attitude kicked in.

"I charge for those," he joked. "And my own hospital can't afford it."

His smile weakened me from inside; it made my pain look so small, my desires so petty, and my anger so meaningless. The sense of déjà vu just grew taller, too. "We've had this conversation before, too? Haven't we?" I raised my doubts aloud.

"Yes, we have." He opened the file and tossed it over to me. "This is the record of our previous meeting."

"Isn't this not supposed to be shared with patients?"

"Like I said, I have developed my own method, and it begins with trust."

I was shameless, curious, anxious, edgy, confused. I didn't know whether to read the notes or burn them. This was what I was a decade ago. If I dug into it, there was no coming back. A bomb-storm had passed, and my will to resist had crumbled.

It was time to know Saira.

"First question Saira asked was to validate her fear, her apprehension. She's already made a decision of how the world around was. Every positive validation confirmed her suspicion and every negative one provided relief.

"Today she asked me whether I was really handicapped or I was pretending to be one to get her trust. That's a unique question. Paranoia is paramount, and trust is a scarce mineral even with her loved one. Slowly all her relief from invalidation of her suspicions went away in an amalgamation of facts and fiction. Facts must be separated."

There was nothing after that. "Where's the rest of it?" I asked.

"I promise I'll give you all, but first you have to let me examine you."

"No. I want to read it all."

"Trust me on this. It's far more tedious to read half-baked notes than to experience it yourself."

"What do you mean, experience it?"

"You know why you're here today?"

"I wish I didn't know."

"You're funny." He chuckled again, almost child-like, tried to restrain, but then gave up again. "So what *do* you know?"

"You fixed me before, and now you want to patch up that work and make sure the coma hasn't made me crazier."

"Crazier?" he laughed. "You were a fourteen-year-old girl when you came here. Trust me, everyone is crazy at that age. Today, you're a lot saner than 90% of my staff here. Let's make that 100%, which includes me, too!" I liked him; and I think I also trusted him now.

"I have one question for you, if I may?" he continued.

"I'll be glad to be of help," I said.

"The procedure request mentions that I have something that belongs to you. I need to return it to you. Your memories." He paused. "You think I stole your memories?"

"No, you didn't quite steal it."

A slight rod of discomfort appeared on his face. He maneuvered his wheel chair a bit. "You and I had an agreement to hide it to a safe place. Where no one could find it. Not even you," he said. "Are you sure you're ready for this?"

"Yes. I want it taken out today." Before he could argue further, I rudely interrupted, "I want to go back to being my natural self instead of this artificial doll that my mother forced you to turn me into."

"I won't deny that your mother wasn't a part of it." He looked up straight in my eyes. "But it was the only decision that could be made at that time."

"It all changes now. As I gather it, the hiding place is no longer safe, so screw it."

He skillfully found a way to insert his thoughts. "And it's causing all the other places in your brain to mix facts with fiction." He paused to take a breath. "Is that good?"

I didn't say a word. I was mad at him now. I didn't want to be disrespectful, but he had just called me a psychopath. What did he expect from me? To drool and say yes. *Oh, wait. A black Pison wasp even tortures me. I'm such a psychopath.*

"Are you ready?" The moment he said it, my stomach knitted together, squeezing up into a tiny *woolzie*, then when he said, "You'll be just like how god intended to make you." It quickly unraveled, only this time everything was out of order, and so was the oscillating imagery in my head.

"So here's the process. I'll slowly take you in hypnosis. Remember, nothing is safe until then. Once in, you and I will revisit a time when we made a two-part key to keep some memories safe. I'll ask you to provide your key. I'll provide my key, and that's it," Dr Guha said, evoking an overwhelming nod from me. "And one more thing." He hit a bell in the wheelchair, and soon thereafter the mirror above the credenza opened and a camera behind it crawled blinking red. "We can record it if you like."

I didn't want anyone else to know my thoughts. Besides, this poor soul didn't know that I had my own camera. "No. It's okay. I trust you," I said.

His face perked up a bit. "Oh, well. We're off to a good start then." He clicked another button on the wheelchair, and the blinking light of the camera stopped behind the rolled back mirror. The credenza and the mirror looked just like before, pieces of furniture.

"Are you safe?" he asked me.

"No," I replied.

"Okay. Let's go to a place where we're safe. Is that okay?"

"Yes."

"I'll count from three to zero and when I say zero, you'll find yourself in a place where there's one big locker room with a giant steel door, and I want you to go near it. Okay?"

"Yes."

"Okay, here we go. Three, two, one… zero."

A white fog ensued. When it settled, I was exactly where Dr Guha had described.

"Are you by the door?" his voice echoed.

"Yes."

"Who else is there with you?"

I looked to my side. Not too far stood his wheelchair and him in it.

"You're there."

"Now let me open the door for you. Pillow slept on a pillow."

A pin drop silence whooshed away with the cranking of metallic levers.

"The door is opening," I exclaimed.

"I have entered my key, and now you're in the locker room. What do you see?"

"I see just one safe deposit box."

"What else do you see?"

"I see that it has my name on it."

"Can you see what's inside?"

"No."

"Do you remember the last time you were here?"

"Yes."

It felt like an out of body experience. I stood on the side looking at my hologram, only I was much younger, so much more beautiful, standing there so confused, and a young Dr Guha glowed right next to me.

"Now remember. I want you to just see, experience, and for a while I won't talk to you." He paused. "Good luck, little lady."

"Now, tell me a secret that no one knows," young Dr Guha, demanded.

"Why?" I replied.

"Why not?"

"I don't want you to know."

"You don't know me, and it doesn't make sense for you to tell me a secret that you wish no one knew. Is that right?"

"Yes." I looked so confused.

"So how about we make sure that no one ever gets to know it."

"Can we do that?"

"Yes. We can. But like any precious thing, we need to hide it away from everyone."

The young Dr Guha asked, "Where do we keep things that are precious, priceless?"

"In a bank. Tucked into a safe deposit box."

"Good," he said. "So we need a big safe and a key."

"I don't have a key," I bawled.

"You can make one."

"How?"

"Tell me something that's dear to you. Like a phrase or a song or a poem?"

"I've written many."

"Can we try something that isn't written by you?"

"Why?"

"I'm sure each word of your poem is worth a million bucks. I don't think I can afford that."

"I don't know any."

"Try just a bit harder. I am sure your young mind can spare one for this old man."

I kept thinking about the only one poem that fit my current predicament. Uncoiling one sentence after another, it started with "Eight angels and a pig..."

"Yes, that works."

"Now wait for me to leave. After I do, you need to store all these memories in this safe and lock it. This key will protect you. Therefore, we'll have to erase the key after you're done. This way your memories will always be safe and no one can get it, no matter how much they try.

Now, I'll walk away. Remember, no one can know the key, not even me." Young Dr Guha walked away from the room.

"I need you to walk away, too," I told the old Dr Guha.

"You found the key?"

"Yes."

"Okay. Good luck, Saira." Old Dr Guha vanished from the room. I closed the main door behind me. My heart felt harder than a rock, my legs trembled with tension, my stomach hived with stress. Here I was, about to unleash a part of me that I had cut out. *It was time to become whole again*. Here goes the chanting...

"Eight angels and a pig
Eight angels and a pig
Let them come and take your toys
But find a safe and hide your joys
Don't you weep, don't you sleep
If eyes shut and thoughts don't fit
Wake up and dig... Wake up and dig
Remember the doll, don't forget the wig."

The floor under me shot the tiles off the pallet. The locks began to move, spiralling down the giant chains, clanking through each combination, ripping open the metal sheets down the black hole. One by one, each sheet of metal melted until there was none. What remained were two neatly packed photo binders, glowing in blue.

I picked up the first binder. A calligraphic inscription appeared magically once the binder settled in my hands. *Pillow and My Poet*, it read.

I turned a page and, before long, I felt like I was jetting down a spacecraft, ripping through the clouds, thinking I was going to die, then came the roof of a house. "I am going to die!" I screamed at the impact point, only to dissolve in thin vapour before erupting back.

This was my bedroom as a child. Amaan and I lay on the bed, our legs humming to an old Linkin Park song.

"You know what I do when I feel sad?" I asked. "I ask Pillow a really tough question."

"Pillow is a dog. Duh." This was classic Amaan.

"I know, silly. I don't expect him to answer, obviously. But you need to look at his eyes. They're all confused when I ask the question and the way he lights up when I start explaining what the answer is."

"This is pretty weird."

"Okay. So what do you do?"

"Nothing."

"How can you do nothing and not be bored?"

"I don't."

"You're lying. Tell me."

"Seriously. I don't do anything."

"Okay, fine. Then why did you ask me? I feel cheated now."

"Alright, alright." He paused. "I write."

"Wow!" I needed just the slightest provocation to bubble up. "Stories?"

There was a long pause, and then another long pause before one word came out. "Poems."

"Me, too! I want to hear all of yours!"

"Promise me. You won't tell anyone?" he asked. "This needs to be just between us."

"Promise."

"Okay. It's about angels and a bad pig."

"Tell me more," I asked. It was the most fascinating thing I had heard.

"This is it," he replied.

"What does it mean?"

"It means that you can't trust anyone other than me. Okay?"

"Okay."

"So, do you trust me?"

"I do."

"Prove it."

"How?"

"You have to kill Pillow."

"What? That's insane." I was so mad, and all he did was laugh.

I shut the binder thinking how beautiful I looked. Time has shaved all that glitz off me.

While I was still in deep self-study, I don't know how, but the whole world disappeared, and I was back in the locker room. It felt strange. *Why would I keep this memory unless I had anticipated that I'll open this at some point in the future and this would remind me of how I picked my poem key?*

All right, let me pick the next one. The next binder. The name printed in blood. *"Why me?"*

Soon the pages flirted with wind, a hurricane swirled the binder away. I had to rush. I fought off the wind, crawling my hands on the floor, my nails full of dirt, my bones wet with muck. I could see the binder; I had to get to it.

Why me? The haunting title pricked my fear but my resolute came to the rescue.

Oh wait, no, what's happening now? *The butterflies in my belly are all alive now.* I could feel their stinging stabs swarming within me, and like a thrust, a giant wave threw me up above, the flies swarming out of my mouth until I reached a height where there was nothing but sunlight. Everything looked so small from here. *Where am I?*

Oh, my god! I was at the peak of the wave, must be taller than Burj Khalifa. I had to hold onto one of these threads, but I couldn't. I kept on slipping until there weren't any threads, just gushing streams of water and now, no, no, no.

I must be dead. No one could survive that fall. I felt in hell, wrapped in a sticky molasses of god knows what. Must be the time spewing all its frustration of being jailed. I feared opening my eyes. *What if I was at the peak again? I'll die of vertigo.*

"You aren't," Pison was back, whispering through her venom. I opened my eyes, and there I was in the playground, lying on the bench, my eyes shut behind blinders.

The young me woke up. I could feel what she was feeling, so dizzy. Why was I sleeping in the playground? In the middle of the day? Pillow… Where is he? He always came to the playground. I've been waiting for Pillow, haven't I? How naïve I was.

Wait, why was I looking up to the black hill? Don't do it. Stop it. You know that Wild Wolf cottage was forbidden, haunted. Don't go there. I didn't listen. I could feel little mushrooms growing in my belly. Poor me. How can I save myself?

A puff of wind and off I went, up the rocks, under the trees, and slithered inside the metal cage.

"Pillow! Pillow!" I screamed. "Don't make me upset. Come back."

I climbed eight hundred feet, threw myself out from the end of the tunnel under a hut, and ran into the woods. The world paced past me, my head was chilling, my palms doused in sweat and blood. All I could think of was Pillow. The hapless face of him wasn't something I could pluck out of my memory, and then I stumbled down into the dump.

"Hello Saira." It was Amaan's young dad. "What are you doing here?" he asked at the foot of my fall. I was still sifting through the dump, trying to find some clean breaths that I could use. I had run out of mine.

"What happened?" he asked again.

"My doggy Pillow is missing."

"Aren't you too far away from your house, though?"

"He may have run away this way."

"Why don't you go to your house and I'll send someone to look for him." He was reassuring. "I promise. I'll get your dog back to you."

I slowly turned back and walked away. I felt his eyes on me until I had moved a good hundred metres. He then quickly vanished into that haunting Wild Wolf cottage. I paled. He went into the haunted cottage. Maybe he didn't know. I turned, took my shoes off, and ran to save him. I had to save Amaan's dad.

"I have to go back. Is she okay?" I heard my mother's voice from inside. She was barely clothed. "The pills were supposed to keep her knocked out for another four hours."

"She did look drowsy," Amaan's dad concurred. "She was looking disoriented… trying to find her dog?"

"Oh. That silly dog always runs to the hills."

"I can see another dog that runs to the woods." My mother teased Amaan's dad. He was sleazy too, for then he took his shirt out. My mother made love to him. I had never seen anything like it before. Why was my mother dressed like an animal and him a warrior?

I quietly jumped down and through the tunnel. I vanished faster than a woodchuck.

I was back at home, but the vivid images hung wet in my head, alongside a weird sensation, as if I had become a woman all of a sudden. I had decent size boobs; I was taller than most in my class. I could have passed for a twelfth grader or higher. Was I ready to experience life as my mother did with Amaan's dad? A thought lingered.

Wait. What just happened? Puffed in a glass capsule, I was thrown back close to the Wild Wolf cottage with Amaan standing next to me.

Must be the time shift. Another page in the same binder.

"Durga found Pillow." Amaan raised his arms to an uncovered grave. I couldn't believe it. I had shed every tear I could. Every step was a prayer, hoping it wasn't Pillow, until it wasn't. A little carcass lay there, along with his locket. The one I made for him.

I crumbled into Amaan's arms amidst the violence of rain, furious to crush us. Amaan was such a gentleman; lifted me and ran through the woods and onto the shelter.

We were so beautifully flawed, wet, and vulnerable. I don't blame him for what happened next. One thing led to another and we ended up making love. I had lost Pillow, but found Amaan. Albeit, there was something else that startled me; the shelter. It was the Wild Wolf cottage!

Time swirled me back to the locker room, my eyes staring at unsorted pages in the binder. *What are these pages?* A binder within another. Calligraphed in bold, *Amaan*.

Why are the pages out of order? Let me put them together. Here goes the first, the second, the third... and now the last. *Why did I put them out of order in the first place?* Is it something about Amaan that I wanted to hide? I didn't want to know any further.

"You promised to be how god made you," Pison hissed. "It could be pain or pleasure. Why keep the mystery?" Pison teased with her crackling laugh. As much as I despised her, she was right.

I must face the truth. I was ready; and now came the thick last chapter.

Amaan

"At least we're all here now." Veer announced as my twelve-hour marathon from Kerala to Delhi ended at the hotel. "And thank you for making it at the last minute. I really appreciate it."

"Anything for Attanooga," I said, albeit shying away from Ria, who at the head of the table seemed privy to every flicker of my eyes.

The only other person in the room commented, "I am glad to meet you, son." His warm voice covered me with comfort.

"He's Ria's father," Veer introduced with grace.

"Of course, who hasn't heard of him? It's an honor meeting you, sir," I chimed with charm, but for some reason, charm was lost on Ria.

"It looks like I'm not the only one late," I tried to divert. "Where is everyone?"

"They're on their way. Perhaps the traffic from Attanooga to Delhi has succumbed to the smoke of the city." Ria's father snickered. "How was the traffic for you?"

"Actually I'm coming from the airport." Lying isn't my best suit. My comment wasn't necessary. The cat, however, was out of the bag. Now it was her turn to litter the place.

"Where from?" Veer questioned.

"Kerala," I said out flat, devoid of any melodrama.

"I've seen your Ski Cliff plans. You won't be going to Kerala for any vacation once the winter starts. This is going to be the Swiss Alps of the East," Ria's father droned again.

On the other hand, Ria's eyes climbed the curious ladder. It wasn't looking good. "Enough, dad. Let's go ahead and get started," she said.

"Sure." Veer took charge of the mic. "First, let's get some breakfast in the dining room."

"CONGRATULATIONS, Mr PRINCE!" came the shouting from a herd of suits, graffiti in the air, music stomping through the speakers and flower garlands snaking on my chest.

"My brother, your prince has done something that no king has ever been able to do for Attanooga," proclaimed Veer to a thumping crowd of legislators, leaders, business council, and city officials.

There wasn't a chance in power ball that I could have guessed the numbers for this surprise. The call last night from my brother had felt like a futile request to move a mountain when there wasn't a river of gold under it.

The festivity of the room was growing like a vine on a pine. Ria seemingly had managed to hide her icy thoughts behind her superfluous smile.

"Today I'm glad to say that our project has led to another business venture. Mr Kapur, and his private equity firm have decided to invest in our vision, too, by buying a big chunk in Taj," Veer declared to another round of applause.

It was already past 8 p.m. In the last twelve hours or so, Ria and I hadn't spoken much today. I felt like a cheater, unable to face her, trying to hide under my skin.

"Hey, you want to grab a cup of coffee?" I abruptly asked Ria.

"Sure," she said. "Can you wait here a bit; or how about I see you directly in the coffee shop? I need to say goodbye to my dad."

We smiled, both of us, at the same time. It wasn't unusual, but everything was unusual for me today, and I had failed to shake that feeling off.

The lonely walk from the conference room to the coffee shop had started to feel like the best thing that happened today. They say when you start talking more about digestion than sex, it meant you've transcended from youth. I'd add to it, if you start looking forward to lonely walks over your girlfriend, it meant that you've fucked up enough. *My idioms aren't helping me either.*

"So, looks like Veer is hell bent on forcing us to take the next steps in our relationship," I stuttered.

"I didn't know you were in Kerala," Ria said after five whole minutes of quietude. She was in no mood to drink coffee. I wished she drank it in the hope that it would cool off her visors. I proffered. Even pointing to my mouth full of coffee and waving signs of how it was preventing me from replying to her question.

"You know this whole Saira story gets from screwed up to a total screw up," I said.

"Tell me more about it," she asked after a hiatus of words.

It looked like I was dodging this well. "I've never, and I mean never, seen a relationship so messy."

"You mean your relationship with Saira?"

"God no!" *Why the hell did I say that?* "I meant Saira's relationship with her mom."

"Oh." Her response had Shakespearean brevity.

"You don't seem surprised."

"You know what I like about our relationship?" She paused seemingly to muscle down her seething anger. "We never hide anything from each other on purpose," she surmised.

What the hell is that supposed to mean? Her suggestive words made one thing clear. She knew something. "Of course." I held her hands. "The relationship is like a delicate flower, and honesty is the soil and also the water." God forgive me for this charade, but I couldn't lose her.

"Amaan, can I ask you something?" Ria's hands were still softly resting in mine. "It will be my singular pride to be part of your family, but that isn't because of your family, but because of you. And I don't want you or me to have any doubts or unanswered questions before we decide."

"I completely understand," I said. "Ask away."

"Have you slept with Saira?"

"Where did that come from?"

She stayed focused on me, waiting for my response to pierce her stare.

"Yes," I clucked.

Her hands automatically slid out of mine.

"But it was ten years ago." I had no idea what to say.

She sighed but her visual lie detector was still on. "You know that's not what I meant."

"No," I replied. "Nothing since we broke off a decade ago."

"Are you sure?" she asked again.

There's no way on this godless earth she could know. She unplugged her visual darts, and then spoke again. "You love someone, and then one day you realize that you aren't loved back. Not that he never loved you, but he no longer does now. Not the way you wanted anyway.

"I feel like that. I'm sorry, I shouldn't. But I do. Every morning in the shower, I try to wash away that feeling, but it boomerangs right back in. I don't want to do this, but I don't know what I will do if this doesn't stop." Her words stampeded through my chest.

"What did I do, though?" I asked.

"It's not what you did, but it's what you didn't do."

"I love you," I declared.

"You want to love me," she said, then stopped, or maybe she said something after that too, but I wasn't listening. "Isn't that the same as loving?" my thoughts stumbled aloud.

She smiled, bringing with it the calm of a forgotten lake, but it was just the surface. The clay was peeling off her mask, and she wasn't able to hide it any longer.

"Can you give me one more try? Please?" I pleaded.

"Don't say that, Amaan." Her words were soft as a snowflake. "I'm not breaking up with you for me. I am setting you free."

"I don't want to be free," I screamed.

"You do. You just haven't accepted it yet."

"I promise, from now on, I'm done with Saira. I was just trying to help because of her situation," I pleaded.

"I know," she slurred.

"Then I don't understand what your anger is about."

"I'm not angry," she mumbled. "But you'll never be able to separate Saira from you. I don't think it's because of something you want or because of what she wants. It's because you're two ends of the same rope. You can split apart. Far apart. No wedge, however, can cut through. You and she will always come together."

"I don't agree." I was angry.

"With me in the mix, you try to pull yourself away from her. That's not enough, and that's not fair. Not to you, not to her, and not to me."

"Did someone tell you something that isn't true?"

"You tell me."

"I already told you. No. Nothing happened."

"Saira called me."

"That's bullcrap." I was furious. I knew what happened, but I couldn't believe Saira would betray me, and I was not going to lose Ria over her. Not a chance. "What did she say?"

"Stop it, Amaan!" She turned low.

"No, seriously." I was adamant.

"She said just enough."

"Well. You know how Saira is. She can't be trusted."

"I know," Ria snapped. "And that's what I had been trying to tell you since the beginning."

"And I completely understand."

"I know you understand," she replied. "You just chose to ignore it. And I, like a fool, encouraged you to help her out."

Her sadness was no longer in veil. "Why doesn't god reward humanity?"

"Why are you talking like that?"

"Don't, Amaan." Her words broke up. "Don't insult me. I care for you, Amaan. I love you!"

She couldn't even look at me anymore. I wanted her to come to me, but it wasn't to work. She kept on sliding away, and her parting words were the most painful. "Don't trust her, Amaan. There's something not right with her."

Saira

"You've gotten the thing you wanted the most." That was the first flurry out of Ria's mouth. No hello. No hi. Nada. She didn't even let me speak.

"I'm sorry?" I questioned.

"Don't be so pretentious, Saira," she blasted. In hindsight, calling Ria wasn't a clever idea. Every word she spit punctured my logic balloon.

"I'm so lost right now," I said. Her silence in return turned into a sharp-shinned hawk stare. I felt so naked. "What the hell happened?" I questioned again.

"Do you think you will sleep with Amaan and I wouldn't know?" She had fired up the bulldozers, paralyzing my mind.

"I figured as much, you slut," she yelled. Her readymade judgment cranked fury in me, too, but I refrained from argument, as I knew it wasn't her fault. It was mine.

"I'm sorry. It was a mistake," I said.

"Really? What happened, he tripped while changing clothes, got naked instead and jumped into your bed instead of his?"

"I had a fight with my mother and one thing led to another." I felt my courage looted. "It was just one night."

"There's never *just one night*, Saira." She breathed fire. "Never with you."

"Listen, Ria. It's important. I need to find him," I pleaded. "You can punish me all you want, but it's in your and his best interest that I find him now."

"So now you've become some selfless goddess, whispering prophesies," she taunted.

"Listen I'm getting onto the next plane from Kerala and, if you find him, please tell him to call me back."

"Kerala?" Her alarms buzzed. "So that's why he was there, because you had a fight with your mother?"

"What's the point of all this?" I blabbered, not realizing she had already hung up the phone.

Screw me. Holy shit. I don't know why I was getting a feeling that I wasn't helping anyone here, definitely not me. There was nothing civilized about me today. Guns were out and, despite all the giants, knights, and Ria, only I could save Amaan. What I now knew, after all, trumped everything, even Ria.

I pulled out my phone and dialled Amaan, again. "C'mon, pick it up. Damn. Where are you, Amaan?"

There he was on the floor, seemingly curled up in his own demons, lying in a hay of scattered pages, perhaps trying to find an outlet.

I must fix him.

"Hey there!" I said. "It took me eight hours in hopping flights and another sixteen in a car to finally find you."

He lay on the ground looking at the ceiling. He didn't say a word.

"Let me start with an apology first. I broke your trust again," I said.

"If wind can blow the wires, the wind isn't to blame," he echoed, with his eyes still glued in abyss.

"I remember now," I whispered.

"That's not nice." His reply was flat. "That's an anarchist creature. We all gotta hide it."

"What's an anarchist creature?"

"Our mind… the memories we treasure is the discipline it doesn't like. You unleash crude reality and the whole world will break its own knees and fall like a furious elephant trying to fight an ant." He paused. "I'd be delighted to trade a few of my own memories for a blank slate."

"I heard what happened between you and Ria." I inched closer.

He just lay there, his body moving only when needed. Even his eyes blinked slowly.

"How did you know I'd be here?" he asked.

"This is the place we used to hide when we were kids."

"Those were fun days. Life was easy. We didn't have these difficult decisions. These heartbreaks."

"I know."

"You know, I always thought I could love Ria. But the truth perhaps is that I can't love anyone. I had flings, but never really loved anyone."

"Don't say that." I scooted next to him on the hay of papers. Resting my body against his, slowly his comforting arms snaked around me.

"I'm always there for you," I droned. "We have a relationship that I don't know if it's love or not, but it's something special." His kiss on my forehead felt like a warm breeze.

"Hey, do you remember Pillow?" I had to find a way for Amaan to face the reality that started ten years ago.

"I do," he confessed. "That was the dog you couldn't live without. So much so that he was on every date we went on."

"Were you jealous?"

"I wanted to kill that dog."

"He did go missing."

"I know... I remember that. I was the one who found his carcass." A treasonous smile smeared his face. "I have to tell you I felt so happy that he was dead." His gaze was back on, and the smile evaporated. "But it was better to have that dog; he was also our lucky mascot."

"Why?"

"Because we broke up after that."

"Why did we break up, Amaan?"

"Those were tough times, Saira," he whispered. "Dad died and all the birds scattered to different towns, different trees, and different weather."

"That's not the way I remember." I stiffened.

"That's right. Aren't you all freshly stocked with your memories of that time? My recollection is smudged. Eroded actually." He muted, not for too long, though. "So, what was the sin that your mother hid from you?"

"Nothing."

"Really? C'mon, tell me! This is a one-way street. I'm like a pig. I don't even leave the bones for clues."

I crumpled a scattered paper into my hands. My knuckles pressed against the dusty wooden floor. "After you left for the U.S., I didn't take it well, and that's when she decided to seek help at Nesting."

His head rested on my shoulders, his eyes dissolved in mine. "So, is it bad or good?"

His arms snaked in, ungrasping the crushed paper from my hands. I shifted a bit away as I whispered, "It didn't help. As far as I remember, I always had you in my heart."

"There you go. You can take the pictures from my head; how will you drain the blood in my heart?" His eyes shone with pride, but there was something else in them hiding well under the white cloak.

"I'll tell you this, Amaan. I'm always here with you, no matter what you decide to become." I stood, prepping to leave.

All of a sudden, his cloak stood stripped. "What do you mean?"

"Nothing," I said in a jiffy. "I mean, whatever you are; however you are."

"Something tells me you're not talking about our relationship." His focus was suddenly darted.

"I am, though," I replied calmly. I couldn't bear to see him confused, but I didn't have the heart to tell him the truth. He had to find it his own way.

"Today is the riddle day of my life. Everything that was straight as a stick has been boiled and coiled."

"It's not like that," I tried to reassure.

He looked at me, staring at me, scanning my eyes, my hands, my fingers, the way I was biting my lips, the way my eyes hid behind the curtain of guilt, all of it. "You know, there's a fifty-one-year Macallan here." He stood roughly.

"Why are we talking about whiskey?" I was confused.

"It's in the Hunting Room." He simply ignored me. "What a fitting name for a room where my own father was hunted down." His pretentious smile wore off.

"You aren't thinking straight," I grumbled.

"C'mon. You don't have to drink. Just walk with me, please?"

He left no room for a denial. We walked down the creaky floor and into the majestic bedroom, scouring the dust off the obscene murals before screeching to halt at the statuette hung on a chain, the disfigured lady scratched to nude, standing akimbo.

"That's Akimbo," hushed Amaan. "Nebulous, isn't it? Just the way my father liked it. Perhaps the last thing that hit his eyes." He just stood there. Breathing through a well, reveling in catharsis. "This is where he died," he said.

I stayed quiet.

"This changed everything." His hands grazed through the fence around. I kept my distance behind him. He needed more than just the body space.

"I never had a father, too," I murmured.

"It's not him that I miss," he said abruptly. His arms swung over me to land on a glass mantle charged with Wapiti antlers. He turned the antlers like a wheel, and from the ceiling descended a chandelier, but in lieu of candles lay bottles of rare whiskey. In its center scintillated the fifty-one-year-old Macallan.

"Let's go back to the palace," I pleaded, closing the antlers. "You can't be drowning every sorrow in alcohol."

"It's what his death did," he said. It was as if he didn't even listen to me. It seemed as if in his mind, he had already written the essay, and seemingly, it was a messy affair.

"You know one thing I'll always remember, Saira?" His whiskers flew with temper. "You went to interview the very person who brutally killed my dad."

"I'm sorry," I conceded with caution.

"Why would you do that?"

"At the time, I had no particular reason. Just a feeling," I replied with grace, being mindful of his increased discontent.

"At the time?" he echoed my words. "What about this time, right now?"

"Do you remember Durga?" I tried to throttle his hate.

"I'll say this. I don't want to remember that bastard." His voice stepped up even more.

"Is it because of what he was accused of doing?"

"Accused?" He no longer cared about hiding his anger; it was out in the open, thumping its chest.

"Yes. Accused." I had gathered all the courage to face anyone in my life, as long as I had truth on my side.

"You know then," he hummed, turning sharply at me.

Fear arrested me. I could feel his rage firing up the coil, ready to burn me; and he pounced toward me, his arms grilling me from both sides. I had nowhere to run, and his spitting fire was an ant away from me.

Several Years Ago

Amaan

The nightmare always started with a rose flower in the feet of god. The temple in Attanooga, though built miles away from downtown, was always swarmed with a crowd twice its capacity. It was the same ten years ago, too.

We were done with prayers. Today's lesson was unusual. Today we read Gita; the right, the wrong; and the wrong that wasn't when protecting the innocent.

"Let's go, Amaan baba." Durga's mammoth arms railed against hundreds who wanted to touch me.

"Get to the town hall!" he screamed to the gathered crowd. "Today on our prince's fifteenth birthday, before the 'blue blood' ceremony, the queen will award you with food, blankets, clothes, and for those old enough, the drunken milk!"

The whole temple erupted in tremors of chants. "Guard us, our queen. Guard us, our queen… " That was the first recollection of my mother's place in this town's heart. But not for my father. He didn't say as much, but his actions squealed.

"It's all because of you," he scolded her repeatedly. Just the pitch of his voice shook me to the gut. I'd roll under the bed to hide, my heart throbbing at the sound of his metal boots. Every time the clicks drummed harder, a chill snaked through my spine.

Soon it became a part of me. My own custom nightmare. At first, I'd hear him in shut-eye, but then it escalated. I could be in a shower or climbing down the stairs or crossing the street. I had just lost count.

My mother's pain was much worse. The horrors lurking inside her. Earlier she'd pad it up, cover it, like it was never there, but then she didn't bother anymore, not in the palace anyway.

"Don't worry. It was a simple fall," she had said post my ceremonial debacle. "I'll talk to your father, but you need to stop crying." Her arms wrapped me in it, and her eyes daggered in the phone, trying to dial my father.

Seconds later, her warm body suddenly turned cold. She pulled away. Her mood changed. It must be me. Another cruel insult from my father for me? I couldn't just hang onto the rope waiting for the earth to move. I snatched the phone away from my mother and laid eyes on a video of him dressed as an animal, soiling the sheets with a masqueraded woman.

My fumes misted mountains above. Today was the day of reckoning to get an answer for all the insults that my mother endured, even if it meant playing with a fired matchstick in an oilrig.

I slammed open the door, hopped onto my horse and galloped straight to the site of that video, the Wild Wolf cottage. I rode like there were no walls, no rooms, no stairs, and no palace. I rode like an eagle. I wanted to be her true son, the protector.

"Amaan baba… Please stop," Durga roared. I looked back only to find that he was panting worse than my horse.

"Amaan baba, please," Durga pleaded with mercy. "Please, Amaan baba; you have to come with me," he appealed again, when I was at the footsteps of the cottage.

My hands were still on the doorknob. I had to make a decision, a presidential one. Whether I was going to listen to everyone or I was going to be my own man. No more cowering. My feet didn't turn back; my grip on the knob glued with iron.

"Amaan, please. Come here." That wasn't Durga; those were my mother's teary words. "Come, baby. Come back. Let's talk."

I ignored her too, and barged inside the cottage. Durga and my mother rushed behind me.

"Oh no!" My mother's shell-shocked screech rung on the walls of the Hunting room. "What have you done?"

"He was smiling, Mom. Taunting you and me," I droned, devoid of any emotions. "I just wanted it to stop."

Her face buried in my father's body. She jumped onto him, trying to resuscitate, but it was too late. I made sure of that.

"Mommy, am I a monster?" I asked.

"No, my child… No," she replied.

"Then why don't I feel sad for his death?"

"Amaan baba," Durga leapt from behind before my mother could answer. He grabbed me, wrestling the gun out of my hand, and threw me onto his shoulders.

"My Queen, you need to leave this place," he squeaked dragging her away. I smiled. An ode to my father's cruelty toward my mother. He got to burn in hell.

❖

"You hurt me." Saira's voice unravelled the naked present and in it was me, the demented psychopath. Her clothes ripped, her face breathing in the floor, and I mounted on her as if she was my slave and I her slaver. The repugnance threw me off her, plunging my soul into a breathless spiral.

My demons had sprouted flesh on their bones again. I could see their blood dripping in my eyes, filling my mouth, smothering me, burning my flesh in it. *This must be the hell, and I must suffer.*

"Not today," came the voice, raising flares, gripping me in the blaze, and there she stood, my mother, whispering, "Not today, my child. Not today."

My eyes plied open, only to find myself in the silence of a breathing bat, and Saira was long gone.

Saira

"What do you need, Saira?" Those were my mommy's golden words after she heard me for the first time after Nesting.

"Mommy." I paused. "I have to thank you for sending me to Nesting," I confided. "Aren't you going to say something?" Her breath was rigid, but not for long.

She shook the crusty bark off, albeit with caution. "Sure. You're welcome."

Followed by a blank dark silence, like staring at an endless yellow desert.

"Is everything okay?" she asked.

"Nothing, Mommy." I couldn't tell her what Amaan did to me. I couldn't rain on his crop, not after butchering his relationship with Ria. It was a horror that buried in me, forever. "I'm fine," I said.

"You should rest a few more months," she said.

"I'm going to take a sabbatical," I declared instantly. I was surprised by my unpredictable idea to decide journey in an instant. "And now I want to take care of you. Just like you did for me all these years."

Something hinted that she still had her apprehensions. *My volatility had become a legend.*

"How is Dr Guha?" she asked.

"He's fine."

"What did he tell you that turned this new leaf in you?"

"Are you scared of new leaves, Mommy?"

"No, Saira." Almost in an instant, I could imagine her cheeks firm, her eyes lit up, and her fist gripped tighter across the phone.

"I'm surprised to see this change in you. A good change, by the way. However, it's like snowfall in June. It's pleasant, but it's also shocking."

I wasn't her snowfall. She knew it. I was the acid rain she didn't want pouring on her, and now I knew things that she didn't want me to remember. But it was all in the past. It didn't matter. Not to me.

"I'm in the elevator," I said. "I'll turn in the resignation letter today. Mommy, past is best forgotten. I believe in it. And you should, too."

It had apparently not been long enough to eradicate the stink of my office. It still smelled of testosterone and dripping tongues, only to worsen at the slightest glimpse of a girl's creaky skin, much like right now.

"Welcome!" Neil shouted.

"You're a trooper!" Suri emerged from under the balloons, the balloons that Neil was holding, while also chirruping, "Welcome!" with repelling obscenity.

"You've taught us how to be a survivor!" Neil's cheesy remarks ended.

There must have been a few dumbbells under his words because all I heard for the next several moments were clapping, crying, more clapping, then a bit more, then a lot more.

Neil dragged himself along to my office, like a helpless dick whose only drag was the smell of a fresh pussy. "Did you look at the segment?" he asked.

I didn't respond. Not vocally anyway.

"We paid a full five minute tribute to you!" He gave way to let me react, which was quite a rarity. He smiled, not the kind that's sarcastic; the kind that's more merciful, and the new me, the smart me, knew that something was off.

"What's going on, Neil?" I couldn't believe I was being nice to him, and not just on surface. This was real. *What have I become?*

"Nothing."

He wanted to scurry away, but I growled, "Stay."

He managed to lift his stare away from the carpet and his tears soon muddled the carpet.

"You're sick. Aren't you?" I asked.

He stayed mum.

I slowly pulled the blinds out. I wanted to see this person as the asshole that he was, not like this!

"What is it like?" he asked.

"Hospital?" I asked.

"No," he said. "Death, to know that it's coming to get you."

"Death will think twice before touching you. You'll be just fine."

"No, I won't." His reply was certain. "I'm the third in my family to get this. It always goes from zero to terminal in no time."

"I'm sure there are great oncologists out there."

"None that can save me." His forlorn smile didn't last long.

"How much time?" I asked him.

"A couple months. Maximum," he replied.

"Does everyone know here?"

"No. Hell, no," he replied instantly. "And please don't."

"Of course not," I assured. "You should be with your family."

"I have no family," he replied flatly. "None which I want in this time anyway."

"C'mon!" I reached for his frail shoulders.

I could count the strands under his toupee. He didn't want anyone to know his weak moments. He must truly be brave.

"So, tell me. What's it like to see death?" he persisted.

I had to assemble myself back and be strong. "I've been there. I've seen that passage. It's not as bad as we feel. We fear death because we don't know it.

"Every day I wished the devil would take me away. But guess what? There is no devil. The devil is us, the god is us. The light in us, when it dims, we become the devil. When it lights up, we are god."

"You're an angel," he spoke softly.

"None of us are," I replied. "We think the angels are to protect us, the chosen ones. But what if in reality we're the devils and death is what shards us of our demons and makes us whole again."

"You think so?" he asked as if he was in the same train with those thoughts pacing fast across the glaciered tracks.

On the other hand, I just held his hand for as long as I could. I felt so complete, but him in this state felt wrong, very wrong.

Amaan

The sprays of rain hadn't stopped all night and well into the morning. The wind havoc marched tall and high, sparing none.

Besides the dramatic weather, I had other reasons to turn into an aimless wanderer in an unmarked car. The time had come to make the long-sought visit and to blow the blue tarp away, to uncage the animal within.

"Do they take care of you here?" The thought of prison was repulsive. The actual site was the foyer of fiery hell. *Perhaps a fitting place for me, too.* For now, I was a stealth guest, visiting the killer of his father.

"Your Highness!" Durga had perhaps forgotten about the roaches pacing under our feet, for he lay on the floor, head to toe puddled in them; crying, speaking, laughing, all under one collision.

"I am sorry. I couldn't come to your wife's funeral." I bent to pick him up, not caring about the filth of the floor. "She was an angel." In return, his face leaked more than his words.

I continued, "And so are you, Durga; always attentive, loyal, and warm in your heart. A devoted husband who woke at 4 a.m. every single morning to bathe his blind wife and guard his young daughter, making sure there was no one in the public bathrooms when they were in."

Every song I hummed, he listened with great care, never once blinking, and not for a second letting the tears stop.

"I need you to do something for me." I rushed him back to the present, where an important conversation was about to germinate.

"Sure, Your Highness," he said, positioning his face straight, but he failed again.

"I need you to look at me when I say this," I ordered, which at once froze his eyes on me. His soldier had come back to the frontline again. "Tell everyone the truth." I delineated every word on purpose.

"What truth, Your Highness?"

"You remember what mother used to say?" I paused to dwell, just for a bit. "A secret can never be out. And now it's out, Durga."

His raisin-like skin crumpled further. "I died the day I killed our king." He parroted the same message again.

"You're not listening to me," I repeated. "You can't protect me. At least they'll spare your life. They'll hang you in a month otherwise."

"I have no idea what you're talking about," he said, seemingly throwing all his fear out of the metal grilled window. Suddenly he was attentive as a hawk.

"I'm tired," I said.

"All that is past, Your Highness." He beamed like an avenger who had saved me from the torture of my father.

"I think you're punishing yourself for no fault of yours." He had seemingly managed to muster courage to denounce my declaration of being a psychopath murderer.

"You're too kind, my friend. Do you know what the plague is?"

His eyes swung once.

"I'm the victim. I'm also the disease. I am the plague. This can't stop."

"No, Your Highness. This is the trauma of the death of the queen."

He tried to interrupt, but it was too late. "Tell them the truth," I said.

"Truth has been told and justice has been served, Your Highness," he sputtered.

"C'mon, you have a daughter. Don't you want to meet her? Do you even know how well she's doing?"

He stayed hesitant, mum. "Look at these pictures." I whirled my iPad to him, the wall of pictures of Bela, his daughter.

"She's so pretty." His eyes flooded.

"She works for the World Bank. She helps the poor across the world."

"Is she?" He pointed down, seemingly hoping she was in India.

"She's based out of New York," I revealed.

"My lord." He sprung onto my feet, wrapping them in his warm hug. I had a feeling his sense of gratitude wasn't going to die. "If it wasn't for the queen, Bela would have been orphaned and sold."

"Now it's your turn to care," I commanded. "You'll tell everyone what happened that night."

"I already did."

"I didn't want to do this, but you leave me with no other option." I paused. What I was about to say betrayed every clay of my bones, but it had to be done.

"I'll come back. In two days. By then, I want you to tell the truth to the world, or your daughter will know your truth."

"Please, Your Highness. Let this go." His pledge continued even as I prepared to leave. "Justice has been served. I'm getting what I deserved." His chants grew.

"No, you're not. Promise me, that you'll speak the truth." I demanded a promise to the royal, the one that wasn't to be broken.

"I shall think about it, if you can please allow me to do so?"

"No," I roared. "You'll do as I say, and you'll give me your word."

He wept through his nod and, at last, he conceded. "Yes, Your Highness. I will. With one humble request. Can we do it after the Dusshera festival?"

My parting consent swelled his face with pride; perhaps it was his tiny moment of light in the dark, cold winter.

Amaan

"Is that Prince Amaan?" Ruckus outside the palace was unprecedented. Powerful cameras flashed from the wall, satellite vans stacked in pageantry, their antennas hooked to the sky, their lights dancing to the thrill.

"This doesn't look well," I informed Veer, who surprised me with his attendance at the entrance, ready to greet me out of the car.

"Paparazzi are like terns. They can sniff a lobster an ocean away." He scoffed, and then snapped right at me. "Where the hell have you been? I've been trying to reach you for the past three days."

"I was in a place where there was no phone signal." The words out of my mouth were so icy, even I was surprised.

"What's wrong with you? You were shacked up at that bloody hut again?"

I remained silent.

"We'll deal with this later." He looked at my clothes. "We gotta get you off this cowboy garb." He swallowed the rest of his frustration. "Get a suit," he squealed. "You're coming with me to the press," and he rushed away.

It didn't take too long for his entourage to dress me up in a royal Jodhpuri. With my face powdered, my lips painted, in no time I was on my way to the pressroom.

People lie when they proclaim that facing the camera is exciting. The truth is, you have to dodge the lights, or else they blind you in no time, but blinding alone didn't make me drip a jug full of sweat. Behind the podium, I sat in one of the two chairs; the other had Ria on it.

A dark, discomforting feeling lurked within. A voice haunted repeatedly, *tell them you are a killer… tell them you are a killer.*

"His Highness Veer will read prepared remarks first, then we'll take questions," the press secretary announced, paving the way for Veer to take the podium and arousing a jostling sound of indecipherable questions.

"We deeply regret the death of Durga, albeit…"

I had caused death again, I feared.

Veer's words marched right on. "He was the murderer who left two young kids orphaned and a wife, widowed. He was to be hanged in a month, which would have been justice in the eyes of the law of our lands.

"As many of you know, our family believes in forgiveness and redemption. We didn't object to an appeal against his death sentence. We don't encourage death; we value the lives of our Attanoogians.

"It's our request to not sensationalize his suicide and let his family mourn in peace; and help our family close the chapter on a tragedy that god may wish on no family." Veer's courage armored, not letting even a drop of his emotions seep in his pride tent. For me, to the contrary, a castle wasn't enough to hide my guilt. *What did I do again?*

"That was really moving," a voice came from the pressroom. "We wish that your family can put this ugliness behind and move on to do good for Attanooga and the state."

"Thank you," Veer replied sans the name, attesting that he didn't know the rookie reporter.

"But," the rookie reporter bulldozed ahead, "My question is for your brother, Amaan." A spark flew in my body. "Amaan, how do you feel about Durga's suicide?" he asked so innocuously as if he had no hideous intentions.

"A man doesn't get to decide when he leaves. God does," I said.

"So were you the god instructing him to die?" The rookie reporter blasted out of his innocent pink veneer.

"If I was, I'd have you die right now." I didn't know that spite cooked in humor was so delicious. The entire press circus was up in splits.

"I'm just joking," I jumped onto the opportunity.

"Let me be direct." The rookie didn't fluster, not on the surface at least. "Is it a coincidence that the day you visited your father's killer in prison, he committed suicide?"

The whole room dropped the whistles as if they had smelled a corpse. Everyone hid in the closets.

"These words are direct from his suicide note, quote begins, 'I have to let my shadow disappear without television. The death will not be televised', quote ends."

I was deserted, and the staring eyes of reporters were here to stay.

"As the matter of death is eternal, so are the matters of life and happiness," I implored. "Today, I declare to give you a princess, like my mother once was. Today, in front of you, I ask for Ria's hand." My knee dug onto the floor, my arm raised, and my mother's ring from my necklace was in my hands, and the crystal words in my mouth. "Will you marry me, Ria?"

"Say yes!" the chorus broke in soprano. "Say yes... Say yes..."

Ria's head turned low and then back up again. She had agreed!

"But—" the rookie reporter wasn't one to give up. This time once again, his brethren decided to interrupt.

"We shouldn't belittle ourselves with conspiracy theories. This family has been through enough. We wish you all the happiness!" exclaimed a senior reporter.

With him, the herd of reporters decided it was time to switch the season. The thunders of applause, the sparkling commentary brought us back in the colours of fall that one couldn't but cherish. Quite in contrast to what I felt, and a whole lot in contrast to what Ria may be feeling right now.

"I can't believe how easily you pulled it off." Veer's eyes showered pride on our way back from the media room. Ria's shrunken face, to the contrary, signalled as if she was trying not to stumble from the edge of a cliff. I felt the same.

"You didn't ask me?" she fumed.

"There was an illegitimate thread growing in that room's womb and I had to kill it," I rambled.

"And you decided to do it with my life?"

"Why is this all so upsetting? Aren't you guys dating?" Veer rejoined.

"No." Ria and I both spoke on top of each other.

"Well." Veer drew the strings of his crossbow. "You've cooked some trouble here. "First, you didn't even tell me that you went to meet the very man who killed our father. And now, you've declared engagement with a girl who isn't dating you anymore?"

I stayed quiet. It was my fault. All of it. *I'm cursed.* Then came the glowing words of Saira from the past, casting a rainbow spell in my eyes. "*You are what you are.*"

Veer's chilling frustration defrosted a bit; perhaps it was I, the defeatist, to whom he succumbed. "What are you going to do now?" his polite remonstration began.

I cranked the ignition again. "Ria, we can..." Ria, on the other hand, had vanished. The ring dangled on the floor, the diamond hiding from its own sheen.

Saira

"He was so young. So full of life." Suri's eulogy had no imagination. It was straight out of a funeral playbook. It didn't do justice to Neil. Neither did the lipstick on his lips, paint on his nails. He wouldn't have wanted his dead body painted like a mannequin.

When the eulogy ended, my clapping for some strange reason was incongruous with the crowd. Everyone was tapping, but mine felt like the stray drops out of a faucet. Lonely.

"Thanks for coming with me at such short notice," I thanked my mother at the wake post funeral.

"You're okay, Saira?" she asked.

"Why wouldn't I be?"

"You two were close."

"Everyone I'm close with finds a reason to betray me sooner or later."

"Not everyone."

"I know you didn't." The roses once again perked up on her never-aging face. "I know why you sent me to Nesting."

"It was in the best interest of everyone."

"I know," I replied instantly. "I'd have done the same."

"When did you know about all the deviant horrors?"

"It doesn't matter." Her affection bloomed through her words.

"He did something to me again."

"Who?" Her brows climbed a precarious rock.

"Amaan," I whispered. "The deviant who got away."

"I meant, what did he do?" Her concerns pressed hard.

"It's okay. Nothing I can't handle. But I'm grateful that you pulled me away from him when I was vulnerable and perhaps I'd have been damaged for life, if he did this to me ten years ago."

"There's a reason I didn't want you to relive that past," she said.

"I know, Mommy. And I was a fool to throw logs at you."

"You don't have to worry about Amaan anymore. Amaan and Ria are getting married," she whispered.

"I feel bad for Ria." The news, though ubiquitous, cut a scar when heard live. I hoped he wouldn't hurt Ria like he hurt me.

"Enough worrying about others. Let's focus on you." My mother wrestled to divert the topic. "Now that you have some time in hand, why don't you write poems again? You used to write such beautiful poems."

"I know. I got to know when Dr Guha unlocked me," I eased.

"Recite one for me!" My mother's request faced stiff resistance, but today she was undeterred, so I had to come up with a plan B.

"Strangely enough, I can't remember any that I wrote. I remember one that Amaan wrote."

"You still love him?" Words tumbled out of her.

"No, I don't." I spoke firm and clear.

My mother softy squeezed my arms. "Let go. We'll move away from Attanooga."

"I'd like that, Mommy. I could use a fresh start. But will you be able to move?"

"Our job here is done. We've done our duty as citizens. We can't perish our lives, though."

I concurred. "Otherwise, we'd die like Neil; at least he had me to speak to before he died. No one is going to sing love songs for us dying birds."

Her face shrunk into a pear. Her eyes weren't that brazen anymore. It seemed the sight of lonely death had chained her in the crimson fluid.

Amaan

"I had promised myself. I'll marry a man who loves me more than I'd love him." Ria's words weren't quite something that a would-be groom would expect hours before the wedding ceremony.

"They say one wish in a lifetime comes true." I followed her eyes to the sparkles of the palace, glowing like a lantern in a jungle full of people.

"We shouldn't be on the terrace. It's cold," I said. "And soon your father's spinning choppers will blade the stars."

"My dear father," she whispered. "Always there to help, when there's no need to help."

"I needed that help. No one could have convinced you otherwise. I know I didn't stand a chance."

"Don't cut your achievements short, Amaan. He likes you."

"I don't think there's much to like."

Her henna printed hands gently hooked on mine. Her face shimmered in the rose and gold embroidered sari. "One that he liked was your vision to turn this place into Switzerland." She tried to rebuild my hollow prestige.

"If ideas were worthy, there wouldn't be beggars on the streets." My hands gripped the rails; my back leaned against the parapet.

"It was worthy enough for him to get me married to you," she paused. "But he's not done with you yet. You have no idea what you have signed up for." She smiled. "He sees you as the heir who can take his vast empire forward."

"I'm a failed royal. A failed doctor. I'm not sure I'm the winning horse. Oh, and I have a lineage of a family which knows how to splurge, without really doing a cost/benefit analysis."

She moved closer. Her breath drizzled under my ears. "That's what your brother is," she said. "I know you will be successful in taking my father's businesses forward."

"So tell me," I asked politely, "Do you think us getting in a wedlock is worth it?"

"Some questions are best left unanswered." She pulled away.

"I know our trust has cracks, but I promise you I'm going to fill them with all my heart." My words drew a familiar smile on her. "I want you to know that when I wasn't with you, I got this feeling like I was chained to a rock, and the ocean opened its belly, swallowing me in it," I confessed. "That's the feeling my mother talked about."

"That marry an anchor?"

"No." Both of us shared a warm smile. "My mother said the only way you'd know if a woman completes you is when she isn't around and you begin to drown."

Ria's brows sprouted with pride. "I love you, Ria." I inched closer to her; the guards of her aroma had already diced my agony. I once again felt taller than my soul. "I do have one more confession to make," I announced.

"You must be wondering why I went to meet my father's killer." I paused, but not willfully. Her hands commanded that I was not to speak anymore.

"That's a sad chapter and it's closed." Her words remained beautifully calligraphic. "Only, I wish you had met him ten years ago. This way he'd have died of guilt sooner. It would have saved countless hearts from corroding."

Her words once again furnaced my heart. I was becoming human again.

"I also have one confession," she said, "For you to make."

"Anything for you." I stoked her claim.

"If we were to get married and remain married, from this day onward, you'd not meet Saira." Her arms wrapped around me, her eyes dilated to test for truth in mine.

"I promise." The bridge of my arms broke, and her defenseless body once again fell onto mine. Now, it was my turn to prove my purity.

"Hail the new queen." Mrs Gaina was the last in line for us to greet in the ballroom. She shone a bright silver streak in contrast to the frosty pretentious smile drawn on Saira. I wondered if I'd ever get to apologize to Saira. *I must.* I walked down to them. "Thank you for your wishes."

"We should thank our queen," Mrs Gaina trilled. "The spirit of Attanooga has already risen high, and there's no stopping that."

"Congratulations, Ria." Saira kissed Ria's hands. "Take good care of our prince."

"I will." Ria's diamond-studded eyes sparkled with pride. Her hands clutched mine. A reminder of our promise. *It was time to bid goodbye to Saira.*

"I wish you well, Saira," I chirped.

"Thank you, Mr Prince," she interrupted. "I can never forget that you saved my life."

"You'd have done the same."

"I'd like to repay that debt someday."

"There's no need for that," I insisted. "There are no debts in friendship. We help each other forgive and forget."

She stood quiet, speaking only through the eyes. "Very well then, Mr Prince," she paused. "All is forgiven and forgotten."

"What is forgiven and forgotten?" Ria's inquisition started.

"Mr Prince's good deeds." Saira smiled.

"But that doesn't mean you're going to stop being good." Ria turned to me.

"Never. Except with you." With those words, we moved on to other guests, but an invisible rope remained latched to Saira. As if she was watching me, choreographing each step I took. I quickly turned around, but she was nowhere in sight, then I saw her long silhouette dress stepping away to the exit. It felt like she was also walking out of my life.

"You broke your promise," Ria mumbled.

"She's our guest, on our wedding."

Her eyes split with mischief. "Okay. This one last time," she murmured while greeting our guests. "Now, she doesn't exist for us." Her words meant serious business. "It's a good thing that they are moving to the U.S."

"Good for them." I hid my reaction away from my calm face. "How'd you know?" I asked.

"Mrs Gaina just mentioned."

"Are you ready for this?" Veer's abrupt interjection cut our conversation short. "Now, you're man and wife. If you like to revel in this day, we can push this press conference out to tomorrow," Veer said, flexing his proud muscles.

"That'll be disappointing," Ria surmised. "We're stepping out for town feast anyway. Let's also address the media there."

"I agree, Princess Ria," I teased.

"I am proud today," Veer said. "Today, we have another queen in the palace who will remind people of the lady luck that our mother brought to this town."

It was my turn to ride the horse again. The guns roared, reloaded, then roared again, and I marched on a white horse. The palanquin moved side by side to the portico. The bearers on both sides swiftly unloaded their shoulders, the handmaid raised the curtain, and there she was, Ria, stepping out to the hundreds of thousands of Attanoogians, waiting to get a glimpse of their princess.

Every other sound muted with the thunderous applause and the relentless chants "Hail the princess! Hail the princess!"

Only a few scarce moments had passed since her debut on stage, and she had already assuaged a crucial hope for millions. She was god's child showering luck on Attanooga in the form of white cotton.

The first snow in a decade started descending.

Each flake raised hopes in the dry eyes of people. The hope of Attanooga transforming into Switzerland of Asia wasn't just a dream anymore. It had become real!

We had to ready the Ski Cliff now; one full year ahead of schedule. Along came the song from a thousand hearts, "My queen, Attanooga's sheen. My queen, Attanooga's sheen."

Amaan

"You didn't ask for a wedding gift." The night of the wedding still smelled of whiskey, and here came the message from Saira. I had to uphold my vow.

"Don't worry. All is forgotten and forgiven." The phone screen blotted blue words again.

"It pains me to talk to you, but I want to do all the good that I can before I leave this place forever. There's something you left behind that night in the cottage." My blood thickened as the words blazed on the phone.

"I understand how you feel. And I want you to know that even though I can't be there for you, I'd never wish ill." The message ended, soon to be followed by a scribbly hand-written note. This was a picture of my diary page. This one I still remember. This was the day I quit medical school.

Dec 24th, 2013: "Why did you break in the shelter?" My mother asked today. I wanted to tell her the truth. But I couldn't, so I made up a lie. She saw through it, I think.

Jan 2nd, 2014: Today my mother asked me to drop out from medical school. I liked the medical school. It was one place where

I felt normal. I couldn't ask for anything better. I felt complacent. Why can't she understand? What will I do now? Not going to med school will kill me. Isn't that a sin, too?

Even though dead, I still hate my lousy bastard father. It's all because of him. He ruined everything, and I have to live in this mess all my life.

I turned the phone away. I didn't want to know that past. It died with my father, then again with Durga. The jury broke the pen with Durga's death. I had no intentions to fill the ink and turn open the cap again.

Then, came the second screenshot. Of a day that usurped many lives. The day my mother became a widow. The day my father didn't breathe anymore.

Oct 18th, 2008:

Today, I killed my father…

My phone fell off my hands. I knew every word of the note, and I had no interest in reading it again. *The note is a confession.* The startling actuality stunned my nerves.

"I'm not going to tell this to anyone," came the next message from Saira.

"Your secret will always be safe with me. Like many others," her message ended.

"What do you want?" I texted.

"How disgusting. Nothing. I want nothing," her message came right back.

"Now I am going to burn it," her message continued.

"No," I replied. *I have to burn it myself.* "Can I get the physical copy?"

"You can take it whenever you want."

"Thanks."

"Shall I post it to you?" she asked.

"No." *I can't risk anyone get a hold of that.* "I'll come get it."

"I am staying at my mom's."

"Can you come to the cottage?"

"I'd rather not," she replied.

"I understand. I am sorry. I'll come to your house. Tomorrow, 11 a.m."

"Okay. I am also sending you the last page I have."

"Where did you find this?"

"Let's not revisit that."

"Please. One last favour. If you can tell me where you found these?"

"It was what you had shoved into my mouth, when you…"

A lightning electrocuted me from head to toe. I didn't think I could rise from this, but I had to. This time, it was to acknowledge Saira for one last time. "I haven't been kind to you. Thank you for helping me. I owe you one."

"In another life." Her reply turned the lights off my phone. I wasn't human. Today I had come to realize that much.

"You are awake," Ria whispered.

"Just thinking about the wedding." I tried pushing my anxious thoughts away.

"Come here." She pulled me inside the comforter.

This night wasn't going to be an easy one. I had screwed up many lives, and Ria had become the latest casualty. I had broken a vow, a gift, the only gift that my bride asked on our wedding night. Moreover, I was about to do much worse.

Amaan

"He tried it again, Mommy." It must be a dream born out of my guilt. Saira's voice was so clear, so vivid. "He'll never stop." I heard her again; her face flashed, then disappeared.

"Tell me where you are. Let me come and help you. We're leaving this city and all this behind," the tense voice on the speaker phone spilled. *She must be talking to her mother, I deduced.*

"No," Saira's voice soared. "This is my mess. I'll clear it."

"Taking the law in your hands isn't going to help you." The voice on the phone was failing again.

"Mommy." Her long pause finally broke. "For everyone's good, don't try to find me."

"They're looking for him. They'll find him soon."

"Remember one thing, Mommy." The displaced cough clicketey-clacked together. "One doesn't like two. Two makes fun of three. When two swallows one, three goes free."

The voice on the phone had gone dark. The tables turned, the shadow marching toward me, the hammer clawing in the air, the life in me shattered with fear.

My eyes split open, my lungs gasping for air. The horror wasn't just a dream. I wasn't in my bed.

Saira

"Where am I?" Amaan moaned. It was about time he woke up. We had a lot of catching up to do.

"What are we doing in the cottage?" His plea was seemingly drenched in mystery shrouding his whereabouts, and I, like a kitten, felt like burying myself in a cloak. I didn't want him to hurt me anymore.

"Don't be a cockatiel," Pison whispered. She was peculiarly meek today. "The wild boar is chained," she moaned.

My confidence rose again, my stripes grew back. The tigress in me thrived once more. "You're the one who wanted to meet here, remember?" My words came coated in granite.

"But you refused." His eyes swelled groggier.

"You seriously don't remember?" *Is he taunting me?* I need to nip him back in the ring.

"Where is Ria?"

"We'll get to her, too. First, let's sort you out." I couldn't let him control me again. "Here, look at this first."

His face soiled in shame as he read the countless messages he sent me, begging me to come to the cottage instead of my house.

"I'm sorry." He could only hope to melt me with a sorry. He must be delusional, for after his attempt to assault me, he wanted to hold me with his dirty hands again.

"What's this?" His excitement of touching me again had pared when he jostled in the thick rustic chains around his arms. "Tell me Ria is safe." He bleated.

"That's a question only you can answer, Amaan. I feel bad for her, you know. I never liked her, but I'd never wish you for anyone.

"There was a time when I felt safest when with you." It was hard to squeeze my disappointment away. "Did you always know what you were?"

His mouth cut open, gasping in dry air. "I'm not going to hurt you, ever."

"STOP IT!" My eyes blotted with red anger.

"Saira." His speechless thoughts danced on his lips. "I know you're upset."

"I'm not upset." My words strung the upper chord. "I'm afraid." I pushed my chair away. My arms came slithering around me.

"Please unchain me. I'll simply walk away," he pleaded.

"No," I said. "I won't unchain you. You raped me. You assaulted me, then you forced me to come back to this shithole… why? So that you could kill me?"

"I told you. I can't remember," he argued.

"You don't remember raping me?"

"I do," he said meekly. "I don't…" His words shattered in the air and fell all over the floor. "I don't want to do any more harm to you. I'm sorry."

"Again, sorry?" I was furious. "You killed your own father. And god knows what you did to the little peasant in jail who committed suicide, and you think you're just going to say…Oh, I'm so sorry, and I'm going to believe you?"

"Okay. Okay. Call someone. Stay on the phone, then once they are here, let me go then," he begged.

"Either you think I'm dumb or that you're a genius." His face had none of the horrors I expected. Instead, I suspected that he was playing me. "You, of all the people, know well that this place has no phones. "The guilt peeled his face to mold. *It was time to play his game on him.*

"Why did you want to kill your father?" I reverted.

All his words vanished from his throat. All that remained were gasps of empty air.

"I have to be on the Ski Cliff for the inauguration of the ski slopes. They'll come looking for me." He apparently drafted a new devious plan.

"Good," I replied. "That's what I want. So they know what a pervert you've been. I trusted you. God forgive me. I even loved you."

"Let me ask you this. You were the one who sent me those pages. Think about it." He spoke in haste. "If I was to kill you, hypothetically, that is… Why would I even fix a time to meet? Wouldn't I just barge into your house and kill you?"

"Try hearing your own words." My blood boiled. *He's taking me for granted.* "You are smarter than that, Mr Prince. You let a common man go to prison for a murder that you committed. And god knows how much you paid my mother to send me to that lunatic hospital to erase my memories of the incident."

"But—" he tried to interrupt.

"No. You listen," I yelled. "Today. You'll listen." A cup dropped off the mantle, enough to snap me back in fear. "See what you've turned me into. I'm afraid of my shadow too." I quickly regrouped my courage. There was no one else; I had to protect myself. "Confess to your crimes," I roared.

"What confession?" He was belligerent first. Now, he had decided to play dumb.

"The one that I'll keep as insurance; should you try to murder me again."

"Saira," he begged. "For all the years you've known me…"

I couldn't bear to hear him anymore, so I intervened. "You know why I came to you after Nesting?"

He shook his head in denial.

"Because I remembered what you did to your father, and I wanted to help you recover. I was a fool, thinking that you've changed. You didn't change. You just masqueraded."

"I'm a flawed soul. I won't deny that, and at times, I can't remember things. When the truth passes by, I see the horrors in it. I need help." His confession had begun, and with it came the violent torture of the past.

"Help? You schizophrenic bastard," I yelled. "YOU VIOLATED ME." I had to pause not to let my face leak. I couldn't afford to look weak. "Now, no matter what you say, it's not going to help you."

"Okay," he conceded. "Whatever you want. You already have the diary notes. That's your insurance. Keep it. If that helps you feel safe."

"I know at some point you'll sneak out of those chains. Now that you know that I have those letters here, you'll burn them. And me."

"Saira. You're acting crazy. Why would I do that?"

"Why would you do anything that you've done?"

He stayed quiet. After a long dragged silence, he mumbled, "Okay. I'll do whatever you want me to."

"Thank you," I said. "And now, start with your confession. Confession of all the sins you've committed to date."

A cart of hasty breath simmered Amaan. "It's cold. Can I please get a blanket?" he pleaded.

Amaan

"Remember this room?" The words chewed away under the creaking sound of the Hunting Room floor at the Wild Wolf cottage. Every footstep that Saira took hammered my brutality of the past, and now she stood behind me.

My mind rigged with prophecies. *Maybe she'll cut my throat with a knife, if she had mercy. What if she chose to peel my eyes instead? What if it wasn't a knife? What if she'd decided to just shoot me? That may be a poetic justice to a schizophrenic killer like me, killing my own father, raping my own girlfriend. There has to be evil in me.*

The truth wasn't far off. I had to end the evil. For evil to end, my death was certain. Saira's arms snaked on my collar, and then came the shiny steel knife.

"Do it. Please," I pleaded.

"Sorry," she taunted as the knife barbered my shirt at first, then my pants, then the rest. The feeling that death is near wasn't that poetic. I wanted to live. My eyes blinked faster than a pecking bird until the knife stopped short of ripping my arteries. A hope befell when I felt neither the stabbing nor the pain.

Alas, it was only a stopgap.

The cold wind did the rest, ripping the cotton off my skin, then frostbite spread all over. I lay sieged naked. The only fireplace in the room lay shuttered, and a knife guarded the passage to it.

"So you want to torture me to death." Not even a whole minute had passed, and the frostbite had begun to peel my skin already. The teeth had begun to drum in fear. The record snow in a decade was about to claim its first victim.

"No." Her reply was still as a lake. "Just uncomfortable." She spoke again. "I was good to you." She pulled a chair to the side, away from the focus of the video camera that was now staring me in the eye. "Why did you rape me?"

"Saira, you know me. I don't prescribe to violence." My own breath smelled treasonous.

Her hysteria was loud and heavy. "Neither the chains nor the blisters have been able to restrain your sense of humor," she mocked.

"I truly apologize," I pleaded.

"You have no idea what tragedy is. You have no idea what pain is." Her fury flared again. "You've been a treacherous monster hiding in that cloak of a face that you have." Her flames of silence burned her words. "Now confess."

I wanted to speak, but the knives of cold spoke first. "I am sorry…" was all I could whisper.

"Confess and I'll make sure you don't freeze to death."

"Help." My voice bloodied with icy barbed wires.

"You won't die," she barked, devoid of any amplitude in her pitch. "But you have to give me something."

"I AM A DIAGNOSED SCHIZOPHRENIC." I yelled the words cut with ice and dripped in blood, and so were my mouth and my nose.

"Oh, Amaan. The things we do for love and life." I may have seen her smile for the first time. I wasn't sure. I wasn't sure of anything. My frosted lips had begun to bleed as well. Only then, I felt a flush of warm fluid touch my lips. The warmth of cognac fumed every single cell on its way to my stomach. For the first time I realized what it was like to die, then be saved from it. Even if it was for a few more moments.

"Feels good to confess, right?" Her ego piled up. "And you get to live, too. This is your," she turned the bottle to glance at the label, "Precious Louis cognac. I hope it was worth the price."

"At least you know that I, the way I am, would never have hurt you."

"Is that your way out?" Her condescending actions were just. "You want me to send you to Nesting, perhaps? Is that your suggestion?"

"I don't care what you do with me." I paused. "I just need to have a proper closure with the people of Attanooga." Life is a bitch. I never cared about it, but today I had the spirit of a wolf to survive, even if it was to write a graceful exit for my people.

"Funny you didn't mention Ria," she mocked again.

"And her, too," I spoke softly.

"Oh, Amaan. I know you. You are protecting her," she said. "Protecting from me? You moron. She needs to be protected from you!"

"I loved you, Saira," I interrupted. "And when I can do such a thing to you, I don't think I can protect Ria."

"Your love was dwarfed by the giant leaps of things you or your split personality did for lust," she continued. "I accept your apology," she whispered quietly.

"Can I get some clothes, please?"

"Cognac can't do what a bunch of clothes can do?" she paused. "That doesn't make any sense."

I remained quiet and so did she, and then she spoke. "Confess to what happened to your father."

"I won't."

"Then you'll die."

"I'm going to die anyway."

"Okay," she snickered, then she bundled in her long fur coat by the fireplace.

"At least turn on the fireplace, please."

She stayed quiet for a while, and then spoke. "I'll ask you questions. And if you answer in honesty, you'll get the timber, the matches, and then the fire." She paused. "So are we playing fair now?"

"Yes," I bawled.

"Good. Now I'll ask a question and you'll answer," she said. "Did you kill Pillow?"

"Yes," I replied.

"Good," she said. "I'll keep my promise." Every log she put into fireplace made me desire life even more.

"Did you kill those animals in the U.S.?"

"Yes," I replied.

She smiled. "Good. See? It isn't that hard. Is it?" She put the burner oil on the wood.

Her matches were out. I was a strike away from life and death, and I knew the answer that would fire up the flames.

"Did you kill your father, His Highness Rudra Singh?" It was strange when someone else said those words. The realization of having a monster within mutated into a giant. "Stop before you say that." She quickly dragged the tripod closer again, and the camera had begun to roll. She waved that it was my turn to confess.

"Yes," I said, provoking an angry hoot from her, demanding I make a full confession.

"I, Amaan Singh, killed my father His Highness Rudra Singh," I confessed.

The camera stopped rolling. She took the card out of the camera and smiled. She knew she had me. I couldn't hurt her anymore.

The match lit and flew into the fireplace pit. The yellow flames of the heat were far away, but my eyes lit with it, swimming in hope that today wasn't the day I'd die. She marched toward me, and threw my chair down.

"Crawl to the fireplace," she said, summoning me. I could have crawled to the North Pole if I had to; my blisters of cold were far more poisonous than those from dragging on the masonry stones. As the warmth of fire melted my veins, a sense of drowsiness blotted with it. *Now, I was ready to die if I had to.*

I must have passed out. My senses squirmed back with an acute thirst. "Can I get a real drink?" I asked.

"You're becoming greedy now." She paused.

"You have everything to nail my coffin. I'm in chains."

She walked across the nude pillar, pulling the antlers, and down came the chandelier bar stacked in crystals of golden tan whiskeys.

"Here you go, Mr Prince," she cheered as our glasses collided, and down came the smooth molasses of Macallan.

Saira

"What's happening?" Time must have vanished, but it wasn't time that was making my blood redder.

"Shhh…" My mother scooted her chair closer. "It's okay."

My vision was still blurred, but I could hear her well. "Mommy? What are…? How did…?" I was at a loss for words. I had to protect her. "Did he hurt you?"

"Who?" she asked.

"Where is he?" Bells of horror swayed loud and clear for me. "We have to run."

"Where is who?" She didn't know who I was talking about or the danger we had our feet in.

"The guy who raped your daughter, Mommy," I broke down.

"What are you talking about?" She jumped with surprise.

"I decided to not tell you, Mommy." I scooped my courage back. "But this is not the time. We have to rush. We have to find a way out." I scourged my eyes, and finally I could see past the hazy circles of cloud.

"Relax, my baby," she whispered. "Here you go, drink some water."

In the speck of this moment, the realization exploded into me like a missile. My mother wasn't in chains; it was just me.

"What a fool I am!" I was furious. My own blood had turned against me. All my bone marrow turned red with hate. "You knew, Mommy?"

Her silence spoke louder than her words.

"Why?" I asked.

"We'll get you all the help, my baby." Her wet words weren't enough to cajole me. I didn't need to hear her trash.

"Help for me? C'mon, Mommy. Is that also for your dear town, the one you said we were done with? The one you said didn't need us?"

"It's just for you, Saira."

"One taunt and all the 'oh, my baby' disappeared from your mouth." I wanted to snatch her face off her torso. "Are you really my mother? We're going to die, Mommy. I hope you know that. And once he's done with me, he's going to rape and kill you, too."

"Don't, Saira." Her face flecked crimson.

It occurred to me. "You're not afraid of him." I looked closely; my blurry eyes were still worth a dollar. "There's only one explanation then."

She stayed quiet.

"You're with him? Are you sleeping with him? That's disgusting even for you, you royal turd sex slave."

"Enough of this, Saira!" Her voice ascended. The heat off the fireplace set my mind in the right spot. "It was the smoke from the pit. Wasn't it?" The ultimate betrayal didn't start today; I just dug my own grave by playing right into Amaan's dirty game. "He made me strip his clothes just so that he could ask for heat from the fireplace. That guy is a criminal genius. But what does that make you? You filth!"

"Drink this, please." Her arms raced the little funnel of milk.

"Where is your boy toy? Is that his idea to poison me, or is it that he wants to have mommy and daughter both in bed with him?" I had completely erased all memories of this filthy woman being my mother. *She never wanted me alive. When the pills and the looney house didn't do it; she was here now, out in the open, ready to kill, no matter what. All her gloss of a caring mother gone, vaporized, but I wasn't going to make it that easy for her.*

Her little funnel of milk lurked by my lips. My eyes raised, my lips quenched, and my head busted through the funnel. The milk flew up, spurting through the room, and along came a long hard gasp.

"What have you done?" she spoke in bare words.

"Sorry for not giving in to your fantasy." Morbid moments could be full of fun too, like this one.

"Ah," is all she said, and her hands raced for my face.

My arms were tied. I couldn't do anything, and in a blink of an eye, her fingers dug into my face, my nose. When they came back to my eyes, they were covered in blood.

"Is this it?" My pledge to live had simply been chopped off my throat. I had to run away from here. My arms fumed to take me with them, but they couldn't move much. I was the lamb, chained to be slaughtered, and there wasn't a thing I could do to change that.

"That was the antidote," she cried.

"Antidote to what?"

"There's no time for this." She rushed to the kitchen. "Mustard, salt, sweet oil, and milk," she chanted incessantly.

It started coming back to me. The Macallan that Amaan had asked for. Must have always been laced with poison. I was such a fool to walk right into his trap again. *How could I be so dumb?* All I wanted was to live, and here I was, breathing my last. It must have meant to be this way. *No one can change destiny. Certainly not me.*

A rush of wind brought me back to senses for a bit, only to retrace back. "Here you go, Saira... Here you go!" I heard my mother's words, fainting with every passing second.

Amaan

"You have to run, Amaan." Mrs Gaina's words echoed with every step I ran through this dark tunnel descending the hill. "This is the only way to get into and out of this cottage right now."

"Why?" I had asked.

"Gods have listened to your plan, Amaan. The city has witnessed more than 36 inches of snow and counting."

The surrealistic moment hadn't kicked in yet. My senses dulled in the mud. The homemade antidote could only inert the effect. I had to get to a hospital.

"They'll be looking for you at the Ski Cliff, Amaan. You have to make it there," she pleaded.

"Was it the chimney?" I asked.

"Yes," she said. "They've been looking everywhere they can get to. With this blizzard and the trees, even choppers can't get to this place."

"Saira," I said. "She needs the antidote, too."

"You have to leave. I'll take care of her." Her comfort to me, her daughter's rapist, made me repugnant of my own skin.

"I'm sorry. I have done horrible things to her." I wept.

"No, you haven't," she replied, adding fuel to a raging conundrum in my head.

"Don't trust what she says," she whispered before laddering me down the hole from the cottage to this tunnel. "She shouldn't have reversed her memories at Nesting."

"I don't understand," I questioned.

"She isn't what she says. She's not to be trusted," she said.

I stood glazed in a shock. A warning instinct broke me from the trance. "Then you need to come with me, too," I appealed.

"No," she denied. "She's my daughter. I have to take care of her."

"We can take her with us."

"No," she replied firmly. "You need to be as far away from her as possible."

"I can't leave you alone, Mrs Gaina."

"You go and promise that you won't look back."

"I don't understand."

"You will. Now you have to leave. Your life is too precious." As I laddered down, she put the heavy stone slab back on the mouth of the tunnel. Darkness was ready to wind me in.

"Remember. Don't stop. Just run." Her words echoed even as my legs failed me. I wasn't to stop. I ran and ran. Not seeing what was ahead, I bumped and crashed, then stood and ran again until I saw a ray of light shining through a rocky lid. With all my force, I turned my arms into hooks and pushed the lid out.

Fresh air felt full of life today. I could see the Ski Cliff. Hundreds of flags swayed in pride, the slopes covered with snow, the snow machine shooting for Attanoogian pride.

Saira

"You've done some terrible things, Mommy," I bawled.

"You're alive, Saira. C'mon baby, get up. We need to go to the hospital." My mother's face stabbed my eyes. My arms sprung in defense, throwing her away. I took the chair, swung it into the air, and threw it across her arms and legs, trapping all her limbs, and with it her evil intentions.

"What are you doing?" she screamed. "We have to get you to the hospital, please."

"Don't you worry about all that." Panic gripped her ears. "We have to talk. You've done some terrible things, Mommy."

That was the first I saw her crying, and it made me sprout with joy. Today I was to settle all scores.

"So, you side with a rapist who raped your own daughter?"

"He didn't rape you." My trapping apparently hadn't tamed her a bit.

"You think I'm faking a rape?" The repulse of her insinuation frothed. "You want to see proof of my #MeToo assault? Will that make you happy? Okay." I had to show her what he did to me. The blood clots, the whips of his belt. "But first let me tie you up." I crossed her arms, and locked her in the cuffs. Those were her bracelets now!

"Let me show you." I ripped my skirt through the leg, and there I was, shaming my own body to prove someone else's crimes.

Not once did she stop me, thwarting every expectation one may have from their mother. "What am I looking at?" she mocked instead.

Just the thought of looking at my wounds again cringed. If that were what my mother wanted, I'd give to her. My own eyes begged for mercy to look away, but to no avail. *It's okay, I thought.*

The scars were mysteriously gone. Time heals scars; everyone knows that, but what about the pain?

"I still feel the pain," I yelled.

Her words sobbed. "You're doing this all over again, Saira."

"You filthy little bitch." I pronounced every letter of the word *bitch*. I hadn't realized what anger meant until this moment.

"Kill her. Kill her." Vicious Pison had begun to massacre my brain.

"You bitchy mother. You know who I hated the most in my life?" Words slipped away from my tongue. "You, my dear mommy. You always got the better deal in life. Stuffing me with sleeping pills. So that I didn't disturb you."

Her eyes drowned in shame.

"At first I had no idea, and then I figured. You were famished for a good lay and I was your hurdle. It took a while, but when I figured, I had one goal – to let your love and your lover suffer, just like I did."

"You're ill, Saira."

"I remember everything, Mommy. Everything you wanted me to forget. This place, your fuck shack; Amaan's father, your fuck buddy; and the secret tunnel that you climbed to get fucked, right over here."

"Saira. You have to get help." The anger in her pared down; in its stead, her words drowned in artificial love. Today, they couldn't dupe me.

"Sure. I got all the help I needed from your books Mommy. You remember your books, don't you? The art of bondage, dog slavery…"

"Stop this filth, Saira," she erupted.

"You should have gotten out of here when you had the chance, Mommy. Now, I'll tell you the whole story until every cell in your body mucks in your filth. Besides, we have nothing but time." Her eyes shuttered with pain, and mine lit up with every word.

"I excited your lover, you know. You could never be that wild. In our very first time, he saddled me like a horse."

"Saira. Look at me," my mother's words dribbled. "Please."

"I had texted him, no words, just the moans. I didn't want him to know that he was about to fuck his whore's daughter. Where was the fun in that?"

"Stop it!" The sound of her scream made the story so much juicier. I could taste her sour shame. It was delicious.

"You're so cute, but so unlike your lover. He never said, stop it. You know what he said. 'You have to be punished for this,' then he turned that cloak, and up, I was fork lifted by the ropes. I can still feel his teeth on me. 'I can't let you be human anymore. You're my animal and I your hunter.' Ooh. Such an erotic nostalgia. I am almost wet again. I could fuck him again, right now."

What followed was a long dark silence painted by the hisses of my dear mother's breath. Some reeked of shame and some of flame. Tonight was the night of reckoning. I had to finish the story.

"You monster," my mother squealed.

"I don't care about that just yet." I glittered in pride. "But I will." Before she could utter another word, I stuffed her mouth shut with an icy-cold towel; words weren't spilling anymore!

"I haven't yet told you the way he fucked." I marched ahead with her sins of the past. "You remember his strong hands? I can still feel them on my hips, the way he pulled up my leather skirt, not too hard, not too soft either. He kept teasing me, oscillating his fingers from one side to another, and then they dug right under my panty. I felt my arms fall in the ecstasy of snatch, race, and moan."

My mother had seemingly turned mute. The pain I saw in her eyes, however, was priceless. Every torturous moment of my life was being avenged, and I had a lot more avenging to do.

"We have a lot in common, Mommy. You fucked Amaan's father and I fucked Amaan and his father! It's okay. It's just evolution!"

She had turned still. All her expressions had been ransacked. All that was left was a stare in abyss.

I snooped to her. "So you were saying something?" It was time to take the towel out of her mouth.

"Please don't." She panicked to see the Macallan in my hand. *I wondered why?* "For the love of god, please." Perhaps, it was the confusion of impending death, which had her harried words jumping off the cliff.

"If god is within us, he needs to take a walk, smoke a cigarette, do something, but not come back. He has no idea what I plan to do to you."

"I feel sorry for you," my mother's voice was palpating as I shoved the Macallan down her throat.

"You were a mistake." My mother's words raced back to the present.

I was so furious that I could have broken a cliff, but I stayed calm.

"You don't like the taste? You should. You didn't mind drinking it when you fucked him. Just so you know, it's hard for me to do this to you. In my defense, I did give you many chances, and all you did was paint me as the witch. It's really your fault. You left me with no choice."

"I'm sorry, Saira. I couldn't save you." My mother's words were drowning.

"Save me?" Her pity made me angry. "You made me like this."

"It wasn't me," she revealed. "It was your father."

"Really? Are we going to play that game?"

"Did you ever wonder why you never met your father?"

Her mouth frothed her words. "Because you were born out of a rape and your father was a psychopath, just like you are."

"Don't put thoughts into my head."

"But you're going a step ahead," she said. "You're going to be a killer, too."

"Killer, too?" I spouted. "Oh, Mommy. I became a killer ten years ago, when I killed your fuck buddy."

Her blood-soaked face swelled up. Her wretched eyes wide open as a hawk.

"You're evil," she barked.

"That's what they all say," I mocked.

"And you know what I tell them? Darling, I ain't killing you. You have to kill yourself."

"You should have never been born," my mother's weak words seemed laced with the same poison she saved me from.

"I understand." I smiled. "But it's too late now, Mommy."

"I didn't want to kill anyone. Certainly not you. Or Neil. And I'll get Amaan, too, you know, if not first-hand, then through his confession tapes!"

Her face shook, confused with a stream of blood from her nose. "Goodbye, Mommy. Here, I'll help you." I walked with pride, doused my finger into her blood and shoved it right into her mouth.

The rumblings of her last beat shook the entire cottage. A loud goodbye before she went into the arms of death. Her eyes wide open, her mouth soaped with froth, her nose waxed with blood, and her bare feet bathing in her own blood.

The rumblings, however, only grew louder. *There was someone else in the cottage.*

Amaan

The chains clinked, and as I pushed away the rocky slab back onto the floor. I felt strangely light, although it wasn't late before I lay strung on a pulley like a hapless fish. *I had walked right into Saira'strap.*

"What happened to Mrs Gaina?" One look at her foaming mouth and I knew she was gone. I had failed her. She tried to save my life, and I let her stay back with her monster daughter. *I was, and always will be, the coward my father thought of me.*

"She decided to leave our world." Saira was flat, no modulation, no emotion, as if she read it from a teleprompter.

"Why did you come back?" She looked into my eyes as I swung on her bait apparatus. "I get it. Trying to be a brave saviour? I'm sorry. A tad late."

"You know your father used this pulley to drag his bitches when they snuck in from that shame of a tunnel manhole."

"And how would you know that, Saira?"

"Because I was one of them." She wore that declaration like a badge. "And so was my mother."

A train of deceit hit me, shattering me into a million pieces of fury, treachery, humiliation, all at once.

"I know it's a bit of a shock to you." She didn't try to hide her pretentious mood. "But that's life, my prince! I believe if my mother was stupid enough to rescue you, she must have sunk her dirty teeth with false tales about me as well."

"No, she didn't." My only hope was to play along with her.

"Really?" She looked amused. "What did she say exactly?"

"That I had to be at the Ski Cliff and that I had to rush."

"Strange," she said. "She comes alone all this way fighting those scorpions and snakes, to rescue you, so that you can be at the stupid Ski Cliff?"

"It's a new beginning for the town. You won't understand its value."

"Stop that nonsense. Town, town, town!!" she mocked. "You are cute." She pulled her hair into twin pigtails. "But you're also the biggest idiot I've ever seen."

"I thought I was the monster who raped you?"

"Huh. You're mocking me now?"

"I have no idea what you're talking about."

"Okay." She came back to her sarcastic smile. "I'm going to make this clear for you, my prince. This doesn't end well for you. So, you can drop the masquerade and we can have one last hearty chat."

I stayed quiet. I hadn't expected this end to my day. My will to rescue Mrs Gaina, however stupid, was just, and if it meant giving away my life for it, then so be it.

"I'll start," she said. "It was over ten years ago. My boyfriend at the time, your father, was where you are. You remember that day, don't you? It was your birthday. It was the day you ran to this cottage, blabbering like a little goat."

The memory of the day wasn't easily forgotten, but I had a feeling I was about to learn more. I stayed quiet.

"I wanted to see fear in your fucking pedophile daddy's eyes. He was an honorable man. Like you, I suppose. He had refused to bed me once he knew who I really was, and how old I was. I tried to reason with him. I sent his wife our fuck-porn video too. When that didn't work, I peeled his skin. He still didn't budge. He kept on saying, 'Kill me and be done with it'. He wasn't taking me seriously, and that made me mad. At first, I thought he was fucking with my head. But I had to show him who the boss was with this Magnum .7i." She brandished the silver gun on my face, and then decided to stick the barrel right on my heart.

"In my defense, I had my pistol aimed at the floor. I wanted to keep the shot down, not hurt your daddy prick until I had fucked him one last time. I had great plans for him, you know. He wouldn't get a dime of sympathy by the time I was done with him." She paused. "You remember what happened next? Don't you?"

"I came into the cottage?" The memories flushed out.

"That's right, Amaan. Your little page in your diary." Her face twisted with a satanic smile.

"Why are you smiling?" I asked.

"You know the best way to make someone guilty?"

I shrugged.

"It is to feed them the story they thought they saw."

"I don't understand."

"You came in, rushing, and in a way you caused his death. But it wasn't your gun; it was mine. I was young, too. Had never fired a gun, and I panicked." She seemingly doused back in nostalgia, then with a light shudder, she was back to me."That was my first sight of a dead body, and it was beautiful. Poetic."

It's hard to leash pain; it's harder to leash joy. I was strung like an animal primed for butchering, and the one cathartic moment that came with Saira's confession dwarfed all the sufferings. I wasn't a killer. I was never a killer. She was.

"You are a sick girl," I moaned.

"Are you hurt? Mr Prince," she mocked. "You should really blame yourself. You see, I didn't know, or remember, any of it until your act of kindness to send me to Nesting and allow me to be *whole* again!"

"Now what?" I asked, well knowing I knew too much to be kept alive.

"Now, you die." She smiled.

"Not so easily." This was my last attempt. I swung up, my feet, touched the ceiling, and I swiftly turned around slipping out of the ropes and onto the floor. My eyes were full of vengeance, my mouth was full of it, and so was my fist. Today, I had only one goal. To stop this menace once and for all. My eyes scanned quickly, and then I turned.

An eerie cold wave passed through, rendering me powerless. I wish I had moved faster. I knew my time had come. The last image in front of me was of Saira standing ahead, the smoky Magnum in her hands, the monster in her flaunting its reptilious arms and legs. Then the wheels stopped, the world turned dark, and....

Saira

My eyes twitched to the bright light of the hospital suite. "Where's my mother?" I asked.

"She didn't survive," Veer replied.

"And Amaan?"

He strained his head in despair.

"I'm so sorry…"

"No. You don't have to be. We found the tapes in the cottage. It's a shame what Amaan did to you and all his other heinous acts. If we hadn't reached on time, you'd have perished in the fire, too."

"What happened? How did you find me?" I drifted away.

"You don't remember?" He then self-corrected. "Of course. What am I saying?" The bulbs of politician's pride sparkled on his face. "You're a survivor. We saw a balloon of smoke coming out of the cottage. The stable burned to the ground."

"And Amaan?"

His lips curled in his mouth, his eyes shut seemingly with remorse. "He wanted to burn the place with him… Why?"

"Who are we to judge?" I consoled.

"Then what separates us from being animals?"

"We are animals. We've just massaged our instincts with a calming balm."

"What happens if we unleash?"

"Then we become our true self." I wanted to say so much more, but I restrained. I had to respect his mourning.

"And then it scars the people we love," he continued.

"It will. At first, then it will all be okay." I was trying my best to play the dumb survivor.

"Will it ever be okay for you?" Veer asked. "You know what? You rest. You've been through a lot."

"I don't know how I'll move forward, but one thing I promise is that the secrets of the past will remain buried, no matter what," I assured him with all my sympathy.

On his way out, he blinked his scattered eyes, perhaps satisfied that his family's secret was safe with me. *He must be heartless too.*

"What are we going to do now?" Pison whispered again.

"Be a good girl." My words were her command now. "Go back to your hut and get some sharp knives." I smiled back at her. "It's time for us to hunt again. We still have a few dolls left to kill, don't we?"